THE NAMES AND NUMBERS OF THE PLAYERS WITHOUT A SCORECARD . . .

INTRODUCING THE WORLD-FAMOUS PISCES—
(ALL BORN UNDER THE SIGN OF THE FISH) . . .

Grady Jackson: Can a Black minister
execute a "back door"?

Jamaal Truth: Can an Arab sheik play
"give and go"?

Setshot Bufford: Can a 5′ 1″ player hold
the Guinness record for the
most consecutive free throws?

Driftwood: Can a gangly white youth who is
perpetually high wear earphones all the time?

Bullet Baines: Can a bald man possess
a Harpo Marx leer?

Jackhammer Washington: Can a rhythm-and-blues
disc jockey speak only in rhymes?

Running Hawk: Can a handsome Indian
brave play one-on-one?

Kenny and Benny: Can identical twins be
charged with a foul on the same play?

NOW . . . CAN YOU TELL THE PLAYERS
IN THE YEAR'S WACKIEST COMEDY . . .

THE FISH THAT SAVED PITTSBURGH

THE FISH THAT SAVED PITTSBURGH

A Novel by

RICHARD WOODLEY

Based on the screenplay by

JAISON STARKES and EDMOND STEVENS

BANTAM BOOKS · TORONTO · NEW YORK · LONDON

THE FISH THAT SAVED PITTSBURG

*A Bantam Book / published by arrangement with
Lorimar*

Bantam edition / November 1979
2nd printing

ISBN 0–553–13087–0

Published simultaneously in the United States and Canada

Bantam Books are published by Bantam Books, Inc. Its trademark, consisting of the words "Bantam Books" and the por-
trayal of a bantam, is Registered in U.S. Patent and Trademark
Office and in other countries. Marca Registrada. Bantam
Books, Inc., 666 Fifth Avenue, New York, New York 10019.

1

The moon had risen to a point where it seemed, to arriving spectators, to be just above the dome of the Civic Arena, and it lit the dome with a nimbus that made it seem almost like a second, much nearer planet emerging from the slush. The latest spring snow was disappearing from the parking lots.

A small amount of motorized traffic was flowing into the lots, but there was almost as much moving on the concrete walkway leading to the gates.

"Looka that," said one of the codgers in the parade of electric-powered wheelchairs humming up the ramp. He meant the moon.

"Yeah," said the one behind him. He meant nothing at all. He was holding stiffly in one hand a small white pennant with a coiled red facsimile of a python on it, the snake's forked tongue imaginatively thrust out an unlikely distance. He was thinking about the game.

"It's full," said the first, still meaning the moon. "Usually means something."

"You're such a dreamer," said the second, "you old geezer. Second childhood. Be lucky to have a thousand." He meant the arena and the crowd for the game. "And don't usually mean nothin'. Just another night outta the hoosegow," he meant the retirement home, "to see these jerkos pretend to be pros." He meant the Pittsburgh Pythons of the National Basketball Association, who, though mired in a slush of their own, were pros in fact and not pretenders.

Their latest, but not the season's longest, streak stood

1

at seven straight losses, and they were at the bottom of not only the Eastern Division of the N.B.A., but of the entire league, and were last as well in the hearts of the Pittsburghers.

A man in a windbreaker with a snap-brimmed hat pulled low over his eyes stood just outside the gate flashing two tickets at the few who meandered toward the entrance. "Bargain here, folks," he rasped in the stage whisper of the hustling ticket scalper. "Fourth row up. Best seats in the joint."

"How much?" asked a younger man with a pretty blond on his arm.

"Bargain. Gimme half what you'll pay inside."

"I mean," the young man said, smiling wryly, "how much will you pay *me* to take them!" And the couple sauntered off toward the arena, their spirits lifted by the encounter that took their minds off the game they were about to see.

The moon rose higher, its beams winking off the slush. It was early spring, the interminable N.B.A. season about three-quarters done, minus the play-offs, which would amount to another month or so—but without the Pythons' participation, of course. The sky was clear, the stars edging toward their summer positions.

"Gonna build me a stairway to Heaven," said the first wheelchair man, still gazing at the moon.

"Well, I ain't gonna push you up it," said the second, "and you sure ain't gonna walk up it, you crippled old poop."

The game was already in progress, the ball popping off the shiny hardwood floor, the sneakers flapping up and down the court. Watching the action was what could be called a crowd only in the sense that it is always a crowd that watches a sporting event. But the spectators were so sparse and so dispersed as to strain the definition. Only the ticket-takers knew for sure, and they knew that the only way you could tally a thousand inside the splendid arena was if you also counted the ushers, snack vendors, fire inspectors, cops, and both of the entire eleven-man teams.

And certainly not everybody was watching the game.

At the broadcasting table, one man was muttering a lethargic play-by-play into the mike, but beside him the engineer was asleep, his earphones cocked wackily on his head. One hot-dog vendor in the stands appeared to be asleep also, but really was just slumped over his tray to lower his price again. "$1" had been slashed and "75¢" written under it. Now he was drawing a slash through that number and writing "50¢— or best offer."

A man scanned the crowd with his binoculars and came to a stop focused on a pair of college students wrapped up in each other, smooching and hugging, as oblivious as if the Civic Arena were a lover's lane. Right behind them, oddly enough, sat a man loudly munching peanuts and raptly gazing at the on-court action as if it were for the championship of the world.

The only other group paying real attention was a knot of five black boys of high-school age. They stared, commented, shook their heads, and twisted this way and that, empathetically trying to steer the game right. "Shaboom!" called one of them irritably. "Man had the lane, just needed a pick. We could show 'em that on the playground!"

"I don't think none of these Pythons had the necessary playground experience," growled another boy. "Look like they all come from Montana or Korea or someplace."

"What you know about Korea, chump?"

"My daddy was there in some kinda war. He said they don't play no ball."

"Well, he might be back there *now,* for all you know, chump."

"Well, if he is, he's got a lineup by now that could drop these Pythons into the cellar of the *Korea League!*"

All five of them laughed and skinned palms with each other.

A score or so of fans were scattered through the seats above the tunnel to the locker rooms. A man with empty seats to either side was playing solitaire on his lap, occasionally dropping a card, which he ignored. Around his neck was hung a cardboard placard on which was scrawled "CELTICS!" The Pythons were playing Boston.

In the midst of this loose grouping were Mike and Michelle. Mike, a brawny, balding steelworker with his sleeves rolled up and a can of beer in his hand, was wearing white loafers and blue double-knit pants held up under his paunch by a white vinyl belt. From the belt, on either hip, dangled a flapped leather tool kit like a six-gun holster. Michelle, her blond hair teased into a tall beehive, was wearing over her full figure a tight, white turtleneck sweater and tight, black bell-bottomed slacks.

Neither of them looked at the court. Mike's eyes were up, gazing at the mighty, retractable, stainless steel dome that covered the arena. Michelle's were down on her opened copy of *Photoplay* magazine.

"Now looka that, will you?" Michelle cooed. "Travolta with that girl. Now that's nice. You gotta admit, that's beautiful. That's class, huh?"

Mike's eyes roamed over the dome and around the arena, taking in the construction details with a connoisseur's sensitivity. He glanced down at Michelle's magazine disdainfully. "You call that beautiful? That's all makeup and fake. *That,*" he tilted his head back to look at the dome, "now *that's* beautiful. That is a piece of real work. *Real.* Nuts and bolts and steel. Look up there, yer lookin' at a masterpiece."

His wife sighed. She leaned forward on her elbows and propped her chin in her hands and gazed at the court. " 'Spose we oughta be watchin' the game."

"Yeah."

"What's the score?"

"Yeah."

"Come on," she elbowed him in the ribs, "I mean it."

"Huh?"

"The score. What's the score?"

"Well, look up at the scoreboard and see for yourself." He flung a hand toward the huge, round, hollow form suspended just under the dome and lit with numbers all around. "Thirty-two to seventeen."

"Oh yeah." She looked up and nodded. "Right." She daintily tapped out a cigarette from her pack of Salem 100s, holding it delicately to her lips between her long fingernails. She blew out a puff casually, then returned her attention to the court. "Which one's Franco Harris?"

"Huh?" He looked at her, wrinkling up his nose.

"I just asked—"

"Franco Harris is with the Steelers," Mike growled. "He's a football player!"

"Well, how'm I supposed to know? Franco Harris some kinda automatic *football* name or something? I'm just supposed to know that?"

"Who gives a rat's behind? They're all bums."

"I thought you said the Steelers were—"

"I mean the *Pythons*. Geez, Michelle. I ain't askin' ya to know all the players anyway. I'm tellin' ya, it ain't the players in here, it's the *place*." He waved an arm again, grandly sweeping it across the dome and shaking his head with nostalgia. "Helped build it with my own two hands, up there on the scaffolding makin' love to all that steel, putting—"

"Making love?" Michelle's eyes widened with concern. "You made love up there?"

"Aw, come on." He tapped her knee consolingly. "Just an expression. You know, it was my work, my love that way. I *cared* about what I was doing, making it happen, putting it together, seeing that what it is, what you see here, from the ground up." He shook his head again. "Nineteen months. Yessir. Twenty-two million greenbacks on the line and us professionals up there pullin' it off. Nobody coulda done it but us. Moneymen couldn't do nothin' without me and the guys. *We* did it, not them. They don't know the first thing about it."

He turned his eyes on her, a soft look. "That's the big league, Babe. Us. My crew was so elite—that's what they called us, *elite*. The best money could buy. And we busted our humps. Didn't even take coffee breaks. Yeah, it was pressure, all right. But we thrived on it. Pros. Pressure was what we lived on. . ."

Michelle's eyes had glazed over. Suddenly she

brightened and clapped her hands. "Look! Somebody put it in the goal!"

"Geez." Mike slumped. "You ain't even listening."

"Mi-chael." She waggled a limp hand at him. "I heard it all before."

She went back to her magazine, he tilted his head up again.

"Yeah, piece of art, this building." He gave her magazine a backhand slap. "Show me, go on, find one exposed beam in the whole joint. Dare ya! 'Cause there *ain't* one."

She sighed and straightened out her magazine, ignoring him as he went on.

"Break our backs to build a temple, and they open it up to bums like this." Now he looked at the court. "Sacrilege!"

"Huh? Who?"

"They can roll that dome wide open and you can see the real stars."

"I can see 'em right now, even if I don't know their real names."

"Oh geez, let's just watch the game."

The game, of course, was proceeding with or without the attention of the spectators. The Python guards were trying to bring the ball upcourt against a rather gentle Celtic zone press, Boston's guards trying to trap the man with the ball.

Gunner Boss had the ball. The press against him was not tight, but he reacted to it with gyrations and wild summoning gestures to his nearest forward for help. That was Moses Guthrie, a lean, fast, well-muscled, and extraordinarily deft ballhandler. Moses loped back to midcourt, took the pass from Boss, and easily moved it into the forecourt. He angled over toward the foul line.

Lucian Tucker, the Python's aggressive, strong, and sometimes intimidating center, slid over to set a pick, blocking the defensive man away from Moses.

Moses faked to his left, cleverly switched the dribble to his right hand, and took off from the foul line into the air, swinging the ball upward from his hip.

But in the midst of that move, a Celtic forward

snatched the ball cleanly off Moses' huge palm and fired it downcourt to the breaking guard who drove unmolested to the Boston basket, leaped, and jammed the ball down into the hoop with both hands.

No particular noise or emotion came from the crowd, which left Lucian Tucker's angry voice readily audible throughout the arena.

"What's wrong with you, fool?" he barked at Moses as they dropped back for offense. "Look at you—you *givin'* the man the ball!"

"My game's off, man," Moses mumbled. "I don't know what it is."

"Off! You ain't never been on, schoolboy, far as I can tell."

"Hey, man," Moses drifted off to his right forward position, holding out his palms, "if I could do something about it, I would."

"Sheee . . ." Lucian set himself near the foul line and watched his guards bring the ball upcourt. Boston center Dave Cowens moved in behind him and reached an arm around to keep anybody from feeding Lucian the ball. "Million-dollar baby, ha! I wish they'd trade me outta this mess."

The sad fact was, the Pythons hadn't been winning for years. Moses Guthrie was the hottest player to come out of the college ranks in some time—not all that tall for a forward, about six-six, but with incredible leaping ability, magnificent moves with the ball— as slick as any guard—quick defensive reflexes, deceptive strength that allowed him to work against the bigger, heavier forwards, huge hands with which he could handle the ball like a softball, and a keen shooting eye. With all that, he could be, with his dazzling moves, a great crowd-pleaser if he chose to be. But he was an unselfish team player. The Pythons had picked him up as their number-one choice in the draft and paid a bundle to sign him. And the mournful result so far was that Moses, for all his gifts and hard work, was far from living up to expectations.

Watching the play develop in the backcourt, Moses, without the ball, spun away from his man and slipped into the clear under the basket. But he didn't get a pass. Boss forced up a long shot that missed, Cowens took the rebound, and the Celtics scored another fast-break basket, guard Jo-Jo White laying it in.

Up high in the cheapest balcony seats were two late arrivals—late as usual but there as usual—two black girls named Ola and Brandy. And as usual they were there with their battery-powered tape player and were boogying to their favorite tune from their favorite group, The Crusaders playing "Put It Where You Want It."

They were swinging their hips, snapping their fingers, and stomping their feet to the distorted music at the little machine's top volume as if the aisle were a discoteque floor. Inasmuch as they were regulars doing their regular thing, they attracted scant attention. Most intent on following their every move were the old men in the wheelchair contingent from the retirement home. They were on the floor level across the way, a position that afforded them a good angle.

If some teams have cheerleaders, Ola and Brandy were the Pythons' "jeerleaders." They were as willing as anybody to fall in behind the locals if they won, but since they seldom did, Ola and Brandy focused their harassment on them.

"Dull as ever!" Ola shouted over the music, hooking her thumb toward the floor.

"You ain't never lied, girl!" Brandy answered, smacking her hip against Ola's in a hustle move.

"We gotta get some action goin'!"

"You never wrong!"

The other contingent afforded a good view of the girls were the players on the bench.

"Hey, you dudes!" Ola cried, leaning over the railing toward the Pythons' bench. Seeing some of their eyes lifted her way, she hiked up the hem of her skirt suggestively. "You like this? Hey, you guys ain't never played till you been——"

"Hush, girl!" Brandy slapped Ola's skirt down. "You wanna get us thrown out?"

Boston took the rebound from a Python shot and started a fast break. One pass went to midcourt, the next one toward the man cutting for the hoop. Moses, quickly getting back on defense, threw himself at the long pass and deflected it out of bounds, momentarily stopping Boston's rush.

The ball rolled over to the end of the Python bench were the two ballboys, Rudy Lucas and Tyrone Millman sat. Tyrone, a good looking but gawky boy of twelve, picked up the rolling ball and tossed it out to Moses.

"How to play, Moses!" Tyrone yelled. "That's how to bust it up!"

Hearing his first encouraging words of the night, Moses flashed a brief, grateful smile to Tyrone.

The geriatric crew, their wheelchairs lined up on a ramped platform just behind the goal beam between two signs that said "Golden-Age Riders," managed some slight, haphazard applause.

Boston put the ball in play and scored quickly. Python guard Junior Jesper brought the ball upcourt.

Lucian Tucker ducked behind Cowens and worked free under the basket, waving to show that he was wide open.

Jesper didn't see him, but instead whipped a pass to Moses in the corner. Moses turned quickly and sent up a soft jumper that swished cleanly through the net.

Despite the score, Lucian slapped his thighs in disgust. Hurrying back for defense, he nudged Jesper. "Wide open, I was. Why you gotta feed him everything? I had the dunk."

Jesper shrugged.

Moses heard the remark, too, and glanced over at Tucker, wincing.

The Celtics scored, with Cowens passing off to Chaney for the old back-door play.

On the bench, Python coach Wilbur Delaney sucked calmly on an unlit cheroot. He glanced unemotionally up at the scoreboard to see that his team was behind, 60–43, and worked his lips around the cigar. Delaney had always dreamed of being the first black coach in the N.B.A., but several had preceded him. Then he dreamed of being the first black coach of the New York Knicks, to be a home-town hero where he had grown up. But that eluded him also. When he finally landed a head-coach's spot at Pittsburgh, he just wanted to make them winners. His soft, pleasant, passive face reflected the dissolution of that last dream. It was the same old story. So he just licked and chewed his fat cigar and waited for the minutes to tick away his night's work.

But his assistant, a lean, nervous, white man named George Brockington, never swayed from his rosy-eyed optimism. A graduate of Oral Roberts University, he had undimmable enthusiasm and faith that the Lord's light would shine on the Pythons—was shining this very moment, in fact, when Moses swished another jumper from the corner.

"Way to go!" Brockington hollered, immediately on his feet and waving a fist. "Beautiful feather touch! Way to go, Moses!"

"Oh my," Delaney said, touching Brockington's trouser leg to indicate he should sit down. "Too little, too late. Too bad he don't make more of a habit of that."

Brockington trotted along in front of the bench, following the action. "Defense now! Transition! Get that turnover!"

In his course, he stepped on Delaney's polished, wing-tip shoes. "Uh, sorry, Coach."

"Sit down, bub," Delaney said quietly, taking the cigar out of his mouth and giving him a cold look.

Brockington sat, though still bouncing up and down.

The officials called a foul under the Boston basket and the teams lined up at the foul lane. Tucker turned and leaned toward the bench and mouthed silently but graphically, "Trade me."

Delaney rolled his eyes up, tilting his cigar up, too, as if he were aiming it to fire at some distant peak. Ola and Brandy, seeing him look their way, increased their boogying antics.

Delaney quickly lowered his eyes and cigar and stared out at Tucker's back since he was now turned toward the basket awaiting the foul shot. He shook his head. Trade me. He had been hearing the same line from Tucker for six weeks now. Trade me. Trade *me,* Delaney was thinking.

Brockington glanced nervously behind and above the bench to a section of seats reserved for the club brass and attendants. He craned his neck for a better look, then stood up. "How's the front office taking this, you suppose?"

"With a grain of saltpeter, as always, I imagine," Delaney said.

Brockington leaned over in front of him, still peering back into the stands.

"Back, bub, back."

"Sorry, Coach."

"Sit down, bub."

"Right." He sat, fiddling with a piece of chalk in his hands which caused a snowfall of white flecks on his blue trousers.

Boston missed the free throw. Tucker went for the rebound, unfortunately climbing over the back of a Celtic to get it. Another foul, another Celtic free throw, and they all returned immediately to the lane to line up.

Delaney closed his eyes slowly. Brockington took the opportunity to turn around again and look up into the stands.

In those special seats sat only the general manager, Wally Cantrell, his gold-rimmed glasses shivering on his nose, his button-down collar rising and falling with the gulping in his throat. He might have been watching a ticker-tape machine spew out the numbers of plummeting stock. His face was red. He did not blink. Without taking his eyes from the court, he reached into his blazer pocket, pulled out a double packet of Alka-Seltzer, split it open, reached to the next seat to pick up his paper cup of soda, dropped the tablets in, and gulped the mixture. His mouth silently pronounced the numbers on the overhead scoreboard: "BOSTON 70 —PYTHONS 49—QUARTER 2."

The Boston free throw bounced high off the front rim. Cowens elbowed in to leap for it. He got it, came down, and had it flicked from his hands by Moses, who controlled it, wrapped his arms around it to protect it, and waited for the scene to clear as the players moved upcourt.

That gave Ola and Brandy a chance to deliver one of their rare cheers:

> *Hey, Pythons, you got the ball;*
> *Come on, turkeys, hit the wall!*
> *Move it like a pack of hounds,*
> *'Fore you fall down out of bounds!*

As Tucker moved past the bench, he paused just long enough to raise his tank top, revealing the message painted in zinc oxide: "TRADE ME."

Delaney closed his eyes again. Brockington jumped up to rush along the bench and cheer the team on, brushing past Delaney and knocking the cigar out of his mouth. The cigar rolled onto the court.

Delaney slowly opened his eyes. "Fetch, bub."

"Right, Coach." Brockington hopped onto the court, stooped quickly to retrieve the cigar, and brought it back.

The teams went up and down the court wildly a couple of times, and the horn blew to end the half, Boston leading the Pythons, 73–49.

As the teams left the floor, Ola and Brandy boogied. The wheelchair men who could creakily stretched their legs. The man playing solitaire and wearing the "CELTICS!" sign, stood to stretch, scattering his cards hither and yon. Michelle returned to her magazine. Mike swigged his beer and gazed at the dome. The five black boys shook their heads. The two lovers remained entwined as if nothing at all had happened or changed, which was more or less the truth.

The Pythons, followed by the ballboys and coaches, straggled into the locker room and sprawled around on the benches. Tyrone circulated among them with a plastic bag filled with orange slices in one hand and a bunch of towels in the other. Players lackadaisically took the oranges and towels.

Tucker headed for the john. Moses moved a bit away from the others, slid down to the floor, and flopped back against the wall. He reached out for a ball and rolled it over with his fingertips, cradling it in his lap and staring at it. Tyrone handed him an orange slice. Moses took it and nodded thanks. He stuffed the slice into his mouth and sat turning the ball slowly around in his hands, shaking his head.

Brockington went to the blackboard and began sketching plays with the chalk, drawing one, erasing it with his hand, drawing another, standing back to ponder it, rubbing his chin. Then he wiped that off and sketched another. Nobody looked at the board.

Delaney came in last. He paced back and forth, tilting his cigar up when he stepped with his left foot, down when he stepped with his right. Nobody looked at him either.

Nobody said anything for a while. Sweat dripped off bodies and formed pools on the benches and the floor. Players continually wiped themselves off.

Abruptly Delaney stopped his pacing and looked around at the drooping heads. "Okay, deadbeats. We got a few minutes to try to straighten this mess out."

There were some muffled groans and grunts as players shifted positions.

"Guthrie, I want you to take more shots."

Moses glanced up, then looked back at the ball he rotated in his large hands. "Maybe I oughta sit, Coach," he said softly. "I'm cold. Maybe somebody else could—"

"I don't care. Shoot." Delaney paced some more, folding his hands behind him and looking at the floor. "We gotta have points. They're dropping off, leaving you open. Shoot."

Tucker came out of the john, hoisting his pants as he strode toward a bench. "Sure he's open," he snarled. "They got a good reason to leave him open. They don't wanna waste a man playin' one-on-*none*." He sat down heavily, looking at Moses out of the corner of his eye.

Delaney stopped, looked at the wall, then at the ceiling. He was waiting for the rest, knowing Tucker.

"My name's Tucker, not *sucker*," Tucker said, raising his voice and putting his hands on his hips. "I know your problem. You think you're the whole franchise here. Gonna call you Franchise Guthrie. You're only interested in playing for the long green."

Moses winced. He was uncomfortable with how much he was being paid, since he wasn't producing. But he was trying. "Why're you always on my case, man?" he asked firmly. "I ain't seen you miss no meals."

"Oh, I *eat,* Franchise. But you ain't seen me buy no restaurants." Tucker jutted out his jaw. "And I drive, too, but you ain't seen me buy no Rolls Royces! And I been playin' a while in this league, man. I didn't start on no throne!"

Tyrone, gulping, tried to wedge himself between the two giants. "Hey, guys," he said in a quaking voice, "why don't you cats just cool it a little. Ain't nothing—"

"Take a walk, midget." Tucker didn't even bother to look down at him, but shoved him aside with the back of his hand.

Moses bristled, squaring his shoulders. "Hey, man, lighten up. Tyrone's just trying to keep us from acting like children."

"Ooowee." Tucker rolled his eyes back in his head. He spread his arms and turned toward Delaney, gazing upward as if to offer a prayer, which was not so far from fact. "Trade me, Mister Coach. Just go ahead on and trade me outta here. I don't need this misery."

"Play another record, will you, Tucker?" Delaney didn't look at him. "This one's worn out." He took an orange slice from the sack and wedged it in beside his cigar. With all that in his mouth, he began mumbling a song. "Trade me, lover won't you trade me . . ."

Tucker stomped around, muttering and growling. He waved his arms and waggled his hands like semaphores.

Moses leaned back against the wall. Nobody hated losing more than he did. And he understood the resentment that Tucker—and probably others—felt at his high salary. There would be some resentment even if he *were* producing. But he wasn't. He wasn't playing well at all, not close to what he could be and should be doing. And it seemed that the harder he tried, the worse he got. He knew about the rhythms and pressures of the athlete, of course. Sometimes you had to back off, let up, to keep from forcing and losing your timing. But he had tried that, too. He had tried shooting and not shooting. He had tried concentrating on offense, then on defense. He had tried to push himself and to conserve himself. He had stayed after practices to shoot and work on his moves. He had tried different diets. He had tried to think basketball all the time, and he had tried putting it out of his mind. Nothing worked.

For some rookies, it was a matter of finding out that pro ball was a whole different game, and for others pro ball was beyond them, no matter how good they seemed in college. But Moses didn't think that applied to him. In fact, pro ball, with its faster movement, more talented teammates, its twenty-four-second clock that kept the pace up and made you work fast for shots, fit him even better than college ball.

Yet Moses had begun to doubt himself. After a while he began to wonder if in fact he hadn't lost it.

After harrumphing around the locker room for a while, Tucker slipped off his warmup jacket and dropped it on the floor, without slowing his pace. "I'm sick and tired of all this talk about *his slump.*" Everybody knew who he was talking about. "What we need in here is a *manger,* instead of a bench for him. And maybe we oughta have 'em open the dome out there so we can see a star risin' in the west."

"East," Delaney put in under his breath.

That seemed to rile Tucker even further. "East, west, north, south—it don't make no nevermind. Only direction is *out!*" Now he stripped off his tank shirt and flipped it away. He clanked open his locker and began pulling out his street clothes.

Junior Jesper sat up straight. "Tucker's right, man. This ain't ball, this is a cartoon." He took off his shirt.

Delaney looked around as the players began to stir. "We got two minutes left. Let's—"

"Stow it, Coach." Tucker slid down his shorts and began putting on his street clothes. "Tell that doofus general manager he can have this job, this team, and his beautiful bonus baby, too. I don't want no more part of it."

"Now wait a minute, everybody . . ."

Other players were also at their lockers, changing into street clothes.

"Hey!" Delaney narrowed his eyes and held up his fists. "Everybody, hey!"

That brought assistant coach Brockington out of his reverie at the blackboard. He glanced quickly around, wide-eyed. He danced over and took Tucker's elbow. "Hey, Tuck, where's the spirit, huh?" He tried to shake the big elbow, but Tucker's arm was stiff. "But listen now. When the going gets tough, the tough get going, right? Huh? Isn't that right?" He looked back at Delaney, appealing for support.

Delaney shrugged, worked his lips around his cigar, and folded his arms resignedly across his chest.

Tucker stared down at Brockington for a moment. Then he grabbed him by the waist and hoisted him over his head.

"But . . . but . . . you see . . . what I was thinking was . . ." Brockington tried to stay calm as Tucker carried him aloft around the corner into the trainer's room.

Delaney watched them go, then closed his eyes as he heard a muted thump, like an object falling from a great height into a pile of leaves.

2

There were only so many antacid tablets even Wally Cantrell could swallow, and when bubbles began appearing at the end of his nose, the general manager knew it was enough. Still he had to do something to relieve the tension, so at halftime he went down to complain to the refs.

Not complain, exactly. More like commiserate—draw some sympathy from them.

"Hey, Henry," he said, seeing the head official appear from their dressing room, "what do you think about the calls?"

"Huh? You complaining?" The ref smoothed his striped shirt and made sure it was neatly tucked into his pants.

"No, no, not at all. I mean, it's just that . . ." he burped, "ump, well, our guys seem to be getting a lot of calls against them, you know, and I just wondered —"

"Have them stop climbing up the Celtics' backs and jabbing their fingers in eyes and elbowing them in the gut. We call what we see."

"Of course, of course." Cantrell followed the ref down the hall toward the Pythons' locker room. "Sometimes, you know, when a team is pressing so hard, they get hyper, and maybe instead of calling every little thing, you could just mention it to them, you know?"

"Yeah, I know. Mention. I'm a ref, not a counselor." He glanced at his watch. "Time to play."

"Uh-huh, sure, right. To help matters, is there anything you could reco—"

His words were cut off by the sight of a laundry cart suddenly hurtling at them from down the hall with arms and legs—which happened to be Brockington's—flailing over the rim. They jumped aside and barely eluded the cart, which whizzed past them, and bumped a corner at an angle that launched it down another corridor and out of sight.

Then, ambling toward them following the general path of the cart, came Lucian Tucker, spiffy in a three-piece suit.

"Hey there, Lucian," Cantrell said, smiling, then stiffening at the realization of what he was seeing. "What's going on?"

"Going, gone," was all Tucker said, walking past and turning where the cart had turned.

Cantrell and the ref looked at each other. Then the ref knocked once on the Pythons' door, opened it, and leaned in.

The players were almost finished dressing in their street clothes. Coach Delaney sat on a bench, a newspaper spread over his legs, reading aloud from the help-wanted section.

". . . keypunch operator . . . real-time programmer . . . extrusion engineer . . . massage parlor custodian . . ."

"What the . . ." The ref stepped into the room followed by Cantrell.

"What the . . ." Cantrell echoed.

". . . Avon salesperson . . . skywriter . . . disc jockey fluent bi-lingual Span-Eng . . ."

The ref gawked.

Cantrell stepped up to the bench, trying to assume a position of serious inquisition, quickly wiping some bubbles from his nose. "What in the world is going on, Wilbur?"

"Huh?"

"Play ball," said the ref. "Court time."

"I mean," Cantrell went on, looking left and right at the scene, "this isn't like it oughta be, I think. What's happening?"

"Happening?" Delaney now looked up from the newspaper. "Well, I think the consensus in here is, we're quitting early. That is, er-uh, we're forfeiting the game."

Cantrell stared at him, his lips forming over and over again the word "forfeiting."

Players started heading for the door, and the ref backed out ahead of them. Cantrell followed them in a daze.

". . . Bingo caller . . . school crossing guard . . . carwash dryer . . ."

It was much later when Tyrone came back into the locker room. He had left after being shoved by Lucian Tucker, sensing that things might get hot. He had gone back to the court and watched the refs inform the Celtics of the forfeiture. Then he had sat on the bench watching the crowd clear out and listened to the epithets hollered down from the emptying seats.

And then, when everybody was gone, Tyrone picked up the couple of books he had with him under the bench, stuffed them in his gym bag, and went in to get his jacket. He found Moses Guthrie slumped deep in the whirlpool bath, expressionless, looking numb.

Moses looked up. "Hey, little buddy."

"Hey." Tyrone came over to stand beside the bath. "Lookin' kinda low, Moses."

"Yeah."

For a while neither of them said anything.

Then Moses shook his head sadly. "I just wasn't pulling my weight, Tyrone. So much was depending on me, you know? And I wasn't doing it." He slid deeper into the water.

"Hey man, don't say that. One man don't make a team, Moses, and one man don't break it. I mean . . ." He quickly lowered his head, embarrassed to find himself lecturing his idol. He felt close and familiar to Moses in a way, but was still filled with awe. Moses Guthrie was the best player he had ever seen.

"I know, buddy, I know. But in a game where you got just five guys on the floor at one time, one guy makes a heck of a difference. And Lucian, you know, he wasn't completely wrong."

"Forget about Tucker. You'll lick this slump."

"Yeah. I appreciate your support. I may need more help than that, though."

"How you mean?"

"I'm a Pisces, man. We need a little stroke from time to time." He chuckled. "Guess I should've checked my chart this morning."

"Chart?" Tyrone eyed him curiously. "You mean astrology?"

Moses nodded and chuckled again. "February twenty-second."

"Yeah, I can dig it. Pisces, huh?"

"Yup. Fish." Moses slowly raised himself out of the whirlpool. Tyrone passed him a bunch of clean towels. " 'Course there ain't no chart to tell you how to play forward in the N.B.A."

"Nobody plays it better'n you anyway."

Moses smiled at him as he dried himself off. "You need a lift home?"

"Naw. Thanks. Got some books to return. Right on my way. I feel like walking. Besides, you look like you need to be alone."

Moses tapped him on the head. "You're a good friend, Tyrone."

Tyrone beamed. "So, catch you later, Moses."

"You got it."

The moon was gone when Moses emerged from the players' entrance. He looked around at the sky. Clouds had drifted over, and here and there he could see a star. His was the last car in the parking lot, and he smiled as he walked over to it. It was an opalescent Rolls Royce Corniche with the top up. He was proud of it. It wasn't just a fancy car, it was a symbol. He had come a long way. Even if things didn't turn around and get better now, even if he were to lose it all, he would know that he had it once. And that was a lot.

He slid into the driver's seat and turned to his collection of tapes racked next to the stereo between the front seats. He traced his finger down the rack and selected one of Arthur Prysock singing love ballads.

Basking in the music, he wheeled out of the lot and headed downtown. For a while he drove through an area of nice buildings—clean, modern, symmetrical. Then the neighborhoods began to change, and he was passing neglected storefronts and dingy tenements of the inner city. Here his Rolls pierced the gray atmosphere like a white knife.

He made several turns onto smaller streets, then pulled up beside a schoolyard and stopped. The school itself was built of gray stone, now eroding and marred by graffiti. Windows were boarded up, and glass littered the steps. But it wasn't the school that drew him.

He got out and walked over to the yard. He knitted his fingers into the tall chain-link fence that enclosed the blacktop basketball court. The steel backboards were bent, and no nets hung from the sagging hoops. For a while he stared at the hoop to his right, farthest from the school. He worked his fingers around the heavy wire of the fence.

Then he loosed his grip and stepped back. He looked left and right, saw no one. He eyed the hoop. Then he gathered himself, set his hands above his head as if holding a ball, jumped, and fired an imaginary shot.

"Swish," he said quietly. But he didn't smile.

Tyrone entered the bookstore, slipping to the side to avoid a customer coming out, and nodded at the clerk. The clerk, sitting on an elevated platform beside his cash register where he had a clear view of the whole place, nodded back.

The store was divided into two sections by a partition. A swinging gate divided the entrance to either side. On the right was the "adult" section, and, on the left were the regular paperbacks and popular magazines and newspapers.

"What's doing, my young friend?" asked the elderly, relaxed clerk with a smile.

"Fine. How's it by you, Mr. Solomon?"

"Never complain."

"Got the stuff back." Tyrone removed several paper-backs from his Python gym bag and hoisted them to the counter.

Mr. Solomon nodded and looked the books over quickly for any signs of wear. Among the titles were, *Science Through the Ages, Great Chess Tournaments of the 20th Century, Emerging Africa.*

"Um, Mr. Solomon, you carry anything on astrology?"

"Sure. Second aisle over, by the martial-arts section. Why?"

"Well . . ."

The man pursed his lips. "You know, Tyrone, you're a very bright kid. I like you and I like to help you. But this is not a lending library. You know what I mean? I just can't let you take books all the time. I don't let anybody else do that."

"I know. I wish there was a library near here."

"So do I—for your sake if nothing else."

"Yeah." Tyrone bit his lip and looked around. "Uh, you know, Mr. Solomon, money's kind of tight around the house. And, um, maybe we could work something out." He looked up at the man. "Like some kind of trade maybe?"

"Trade? Depends. What're you offering?"

"Well, uh . . ." Tyrone worked his lips around thoughtfully. "Oh! Terrific, believe me! I got something. What a deal!" He reached into his jacket pocket. "Four courtside seats for the Pythons-Knicks!" He held up the tickets.

Mr. Solomon laughed and playfully swatted them away.

"Come on, Earl the Pearl and everything!" Tyrone said.

"Yeah, yeah." Solomon continued chuckling. "Not worth spending an evening. Forget the tickets. Go ahead, take what you need. But you know the rule. You mark 'em, you bought 'em."

"Right!" Tyrone brightened immediately and slapped the heel of his hand into his other palm. "Super! Thank you. I'll treat 'em like gold!"

"Treat them like books, I'll be happy. Listen, Tyrone." He leaned across the counter and smiled down. "Don't noise it around, okay? This kind of thing is just between you and me, okay?"

"Yes, *sir!*"

When Tyrone left the shop, he was carrying five paperbacks on astrology. He knelt on the sidewalk to put them in his gym bag, then changed his mind. His curiosity was overpowering. He moved over under a streetlight and began scanning some of the pages. After a while he started walking, still with his nose in the books.

He walked into a fence, and reflexively covered up the books to keep them from damage. But it wasn't a fence. It was a sandwich board being worn by a man with shaggy hair dressed in a dirty trenchcoat.

Tyrone stepped quickly back. "Sorry."

"Nothing at all. But look, kid, if you ain't gonna let the stars guide you, at least let your eyes do it. Your nose will last a lot longer."

Tyrone chuckled embarrassedly as he read the message on the sandwich board: "Mona Mondieu—Astrological Forecasts. Let the Stars Guide Your Future."

"Yeah," Tyrone said, "I was just reading about that stuff."

"Let Mona do it for you," the man said, continuing past and then turning up a flight of stairs toward a door marked "Mona's Astrological Temple." He looked back over his shoulder. "She's good, and more important, she's cheap."

"Thanks." Tyrone waved. "I'd rather read." But, taking at least some of the man's advice, Tyrone stuffed the books into his bag and hurried on toward home.

The small, third-floor walk-up he shared with his older sister Toby was cleaner, neater, and brighter than the tenement building itself. The rooms were sparsely furnished but the walls were painted bright white, the windows were clean, and several small plants warmed the place with color. Tyrone and Toby had fixed it up together.

In the living room, the small black-and-white TV was tuned in to the 11 p.m. newscast.

". . . pinning her trainer to the wall until divers were able to lure Moby away with a bucket of mackerel," the anchorman was saying. "Aquarium officials said it was the first time they had known of such an incident with a killer whale in captivity. And now here's the man with all the sports, the sportsman— Murray Sports."

The anchorman turned rather grandly to a strudy, blond man seated at an adjacent desk, wearing a bright checked blazer and wiggling a sheaf of papers in his hands. "Thanks, Phil," he said. "Well, it was a dark day in the world of sports—especially for Python fans. Get this . . ." he smiled sardonically at the camera, ". . . those perennial cellar-dwellers of the league actually forfeited a game tonight. That's right, I said *forfeited*. And it wasn't as if they *had* to. The Celtics were destroying them anyway. Supposed superstar Moses Guthrie continued his slump, which seems more and more to be a way of life . . ."

As Tyrone was not home yet, Toby was the only one around to hear this, and she was not listening. She was in the kitchen madly working a plunger up and down over the clogged drain of the sink.

"Have *mercy*," she moaned as water slopped onto her blouse. She wiped her face with the back of her rubber-gloved hand and took a few deep breaths before resuming.

Even with her hair wound up in a bandanna, and her clothes stained with grimy, sudsy dishwater, she was an attractive young woman. She was lean, with a face displaying high cheekbones and large, dark eyes. And beyond her nervous anger and frustration about the drain, she emitted an elemental vitality that attracted people to her.

As she returned to her task, squishing the plunger up and down, she didn't hear Tyrone come into the apartment. And as Tyrone had buried his head again in his books immediately upon starting up the stairwell in the building, and maintained that concentration when he came in, he didn't hear Toby working in the kitchen.

He turned down the hallway toward his room.

"Ty-rone?"

Still not hearing her, he went into his room and with one arm mechanically swept clear a space at his small desk and sat down to continue reading his first astrology volume, *Write Your Own Horoscope*.

"Tyrone?" Toby leaned in the bedroom door. He didn't react. "Say there, young Einstein, if I'm not interrupting some great thought, maybe you could put your brain on hold a couple of minutes. I need a hand in the kitchen—strictly physical work."

He nodded as if he were listening, which he wasn't. "Hey, Sis, dig this." Without even looking up, he read aloud, " 'Horoscopes are frequently set up by astrologers for corporations, politicians, even whole nations.' Everybody uses charts, Toby. They can predict prosperity and famine and *everything*. What times to avoid certain stuff, what times to do certain stuff—all depending upon exactly when you were born and the positions of the planets and signs of the zodiac and cusps and houses and mathematics . . ."

"Hey, Tyrone—"

" . . . and still with all that you got a chance to make choices for your own life by avoiding certain stuff at certain times and . . ."

"Tyrone."

"Wow, Sis, this is gettin' into some deep—"

"Tyrone!"

"Huh?" He turned to look at her, blinking as if just waking up.

She lowered her head briefly to hide her smile.

Tyrone was surrounded in his small room by things that suggested the range of his inquisitive, energetic mind. One wall poster depicted Malcolm X speaking from a rostrum. Another was from the Fischer-Spassky chess matches in Iceland. A third item on the wall was an eight-by-ten glossy photograph of Moses Guthrie, autographed by Moses: "For Tyrone, my friend who is on his way."

On one side of Tyrone's desk, precariously dangling over the edge after he had shoved stuff aside for his reading, was a balsa wood model of a Buckminster Fuller geodesic dome. On the other side was a stack of comic books. Tyrone's interests were eclectic—a blend of sophistication and youthfulness. But they were most definitely *interests*.

"Hey, Toby," he said, returning to his book, "I'm really onto something here."

Suddenly the plunger plopped down right in front of his face and was lifted away, carrying the book with it.

"Hey!"

"Hey yourself," Toby said, holding the book out of reach on the end of the plunger. "What I want you to get onto is out in the kitchen. I think one of your old funky sweatsocks is stuck in my drain."

"Hey, come on." He tried to snatch the book back, but she held it high near the ceiling. "Toby, this is important," Tyrone said. "We got something here. This could do for basketball what the light bulb did for night baseball. Can you dig?"

"The light bulb did the same thing for indoor basketball, but . . ." she dropped back down on the bed and lay the plunger beside her, ". . . yeah, honey, I dig. But Tyrone, I also dig that I'm committing slow suicide down at that plant every day. What for?" She gazed at the ceiling. "So maybe someday we can move out of this dump."

"It ain't a dump, Sis." Tyrone sat down next to her and patted her arm. "It's actually pretty good, except for the building and the neighborhood. But believe me, Toby, I know what you're saying, about the plant. Tough work and long hours. That's your thing, being a Capricorn."

"Meaning?"

"Such a heavy trip sometimes, all practical and serious and worried about providing."

"Come on, get serious with me for a minute."

He plucked his book off the plunger, causing a sound like a wet kiss as the suction was released. "I am serious. Right here." He tapped the book. "Astrology. There's something in this, I know. Something in here to turn the team around."

"The team!" Her eyes flashed angrily. "I wanna get some help, and you give me the team. What about *this* team—you and me?"

"Naturally I wanna help you and—"

"Sure, it's beautiful." She sat up and clasped her hands on her knees and stared down at them. "I love the way your mind's full of ideas, inventions, plans—I really do. Honey, I don't want to take that away from you, not now, not ever. But this family got no man, no momma. Just you and me. And the load on this end—well, I don't want to be a crybaby, but it gets heavy sometimes."

"Yeah, I'm hip." He reached for the plunger. "I'll fix that—"

"Nope." She took it away and got up. "Your load is school. That's what this is all about. And never mind about the drain. By the time you're back on planet Earth, I'll have it fixed myself."

She backed out, feigning annoyance.

Ordinarily Tyrone would have gone on insisting that he help her. He really thought she worked too hard, and he knew that her main concern was for him, but he was so absorbed by his reading that, as soon as she was gone, he leaped back to his desk and drew his stack of books to him.

" 'Astrology is yoga of the mind. . . .' " he read to himself, " ' . . . Energy field created by the planets . . . female is symbolized by the moon . . . stars incline but do not impel. . . . Roots in the lore of Israel 5,000 years ago . . . zodiac divided into twelve houses . . . position of sun in the horoscope reveals the nature of an individual's will . . . moon relates to the unconscious . . . Uranus is the planet of sudden change. . . All endings lead only to new experiences . . .' "

And so it went, he read on and on, mumbling, shaking his head, nodding, tracing his finger under certain lines, turning page after page in book after book . . .

There was a knock on his door. Tyrone was jolted upright in the chair, realizing that he'd fallen asleep at the desk. It was light.

"Tyrone? You up yet?"

He blinked quickly several times, looked around, jumped over to the bed, and quickly mussed it up to look as if it had been slept in. "Yeah, Sis."

She opened the door and peeked in. "I gotta get my bus now." She wrinkled up her nose. "You're gonna wear the same shirt from yesterday? I ironed last night, so you can change. See you tonight. Don't you be late for school now."

"Nope."

"Countin' on you."

"You got it, Sis."

She waved good-bye, and he listened to her walk through the apartment and out the door.

Then he sagged down onto the bed and really tried to wake up. "Whew! Stuff really grabbed onto me. Hope I can remember everything."

Moses Guthrie's high-rise condominium afforded an incredible view over the city, and the sun shone brightly in the large living-room windows. Moses had furnished the place sparingly but expensively—a lot of chrome and leather and wall hangings of fabrics in grays, browns, and blacks.

And he was dressed in leather, a suit of brown trimmed in black, and black boots. It was an audacious attire that would challenge the sensibilities of many people; on him—tall and lean and broad shouldered with a proud bearing—it was magnificent. As with his game, when he was on, he had style. He was about to go out to check on some business-investment possibilities with his accountant.

The intercom buzzed from downstairs and Moses walked through the kitchen to answer it. "Yes?" he asked.

"Your car is ready—*sir.*"

He couldn't place the voice, let alone the message. "What are you talking about?"

"If you're ready to come down, the car is waiting."

"What?" Moses scratched his head.

"Very good, sir." The intercom went dead, "Better

believe I'm coming down," Moses muttered anxiously, grabbing his long leather coat as he headed for the door.

He hustled through the lobby, his eyebrows knit in uneasy anticipation, and out onto the landscaped driveway that arced to the building entrance.

There was his car, all right, the unmistakable milky white Rolls with his monogram in discreet, small letters on the door. Behind the wheel, his head surprisingly high in the window, sat Tyrone.

Tyrone nodded to him with proper and almost professional deference, squirming a bit for comfort atop the stack of telephone books that elevated him. He was dressed in a dark suit and white shirt and dark tie.

Moses stopped short and gaped. Tyrone rolled the window down. "Tyrone, what are you doing?"

"Driving for you, sir." Tyrone did not crack a smile.

"What?"

"Well, hoping to prove you a point, Moses. Come on."

"Only point you gonna prove is that I ain't always the sweet mellow dude everybody makes me out." He glared at Tyrone. "Move over."

"Let me drive, okay? I got a real point to this." He motioned Moses around to the passenger side. "Please?"

Moses cocked his head, but went around to slide in beside Tyrone.

"Give me a chance to explain, okay?" Tyrone said as Moses slammed the door.

"First thing you gonna explain is how you got my car outta my garage. How'd you get past the valets?"

"Well," Tyrone smiled shyly and a little proudly, "they leave the keys in 'em, right? Nobody paid me no mind slipping down to the fourth level. And I just started her up and blew dust right past 'em. They may ask you about it later."

"I may ask *them,* little buddy, a few questions about security down there," Moses said, cooling down. Tyrone was eyeing him questioningly. "All right, my man. You're in the driver's seat. Run it by me."

Tyrone nodded once with confidence. "You know, Moses, I can deal with these wheels."

"Yeah, since you got her this far. So how come we're not movin' out?"

"We ain't movin' for the same reason the Pythons ain't moving!"

Moses grunted. "If I could handle the Pythons the way I can handle this hog, we'd be moving."

"That ain't it."

"No? So what's *it?* What're you talking about?"

"About *teamwork!"*

"Okay, okay. Tell me something about teamwork that I don't already know."

"Well, you know about teamwork, all right. But I got another angle on it for you." He reached for the ignition and cranked it on. "I gotta borrow your feet for this part."

"My feet?" Moses looked down at his boots. "Come on, Tyrone, I got things to do."

"You work the pedals and I'll steer."

"What?" Moses rolled up his eyes.

"Pilot to co-pilot," Tyrone said, adopting a deeper voice, "hit the gas!"

"Lordy." He slid his left foot over and applied gentle pressure to the accelerator. The Corniche bucked slightly, then slowly rolled around the bend in the driveway and out onto the street.

"Now!" Tyrone slapped the wheel. "You know what we got here?"

A car passed close, and Moses restrained himself from grabbing the wheel. "What we got here is one supposed-to-be-adult contributing to the delinquency of one supposed-to-be-minor."

"Yeah, you're right—*contributing.* Exactly." Tyrone steered away from a close brush with the curb. "'Cause we're working as a team. *We* work good as a team. So how come the Pythons don't work good as us?"

"Ooof." This time Moses grabbed the wheel briefly to avoid a head-on. "You answer that question, you got yourself a job as a coach. The Pythons are lacking one—along with a team."

"I *do* know why. It's very clear." Tyrone risked taking his eyes away from the road for a second to fix his look on Moses. "It's because they're astrologically incompatible!"

"Say what?"

"The zodiac, man! Twelve constellations, twelve signs of the zodiac, paths of the planets and the sun and the moon! You're the one that pulled my coat. Last night—talking about your Pisces trip."

"Man oh man. I didn't mean no trip. Zodiac?"

"Yup. Astrology."

"That's what this is all about? I hope you got more than that." Moses licked his lips pensively. "Listen, Tyrone, you got to understand that sometimes I get low. I got a tendency to get down on myself. But I didn't mean—"

"I *know* that. You Pisces are always getting on your own case. Like artists, writers. 'Garbage pail of the zodiac,' they sometimes call the Pisces sign. Twelfth sign of the zodiac—the *last*. And sometimes the hardest for those born under it. Ruled by Neptune and Jupiter. May get luck and success and wisdom, but may also get confused and daydreamy and down. Get all sad and worthless and mopey feeling and all that— depressed. That's the garbage pail part. Leave a Pisces alone, he can create some incredible garbage for himself. Needs support. On the other hand, when you get it together, *zow!*"

"Well, if this here Pisces can't cope," Moses tapped his thumb against his chest, "maybe he oughta turn in his number."

"No way, man. You ain't a quitter. And as far as basketball is concerned, you're an artist—a *lover,* man."

Moses chuckled gruffly.

"Truth." Tyrone held up his hand. "See, you got it all backwards. Tryin' to do it on your own, takin' all the responsibility. That's wrong, especially for a Pisces. What we got to do is surround you with cats on the same plane—"

"Watch it, man!" Moses closed his eyes as they barely avoided a dog.

"Got it, got it," Tyrone said, spinning the wheel. "Listen now. You're a Pisces. That's fine. But what *else* we got now doesn't make sense."

"What else we got?"

"Four Leos, two Geminis, couple of Capricorns, Virgos—just doesn't make cosmic sense."

"What we also got, little buddy, is a situation that right now doesn't make *basketball* sense, whatever sign. We ain't got five guys that can play together."

"That's *it!* We gotta have Pisces! You gotta be surrounded by Pisces—it's all in the signs and calculations that I been figuring."

"Slow down. Your head, I mean. This is too weird. You sound like you're hustling a product no owner's gonna buy."

"Not just any owner, maybe. Different clubs got different problems. But look at it this way. All the other cats on the Pythons are crying to be traded. Those guys are ready to *pay* old Tilson to cut 'em loose. Quitting in the middle of a game!"

"Yeah, that wasn't too cool."

"Right. But they already showed their hand, made their play. So that leaves you. You *are* the franchise."

"Listen now, it was never my idea to call myself—"

"In straight-ahead real terms, Moses. You're what's left. So you are the franchise. Dig?"

"Okay, that way."

"So play this on your head tubes: you got this bunch of chickens—a rooster and some hens, dig?"

"I know what chickens are, Tyrone."

"Serious now, just dig it. Nothing's really wrong with the chickens, nothing's really wrong with the rooster. They just don't get along. So what do you do?"

"Try hamsters?"

"Come on, Moses, serious."

"Okay. So what do you do with your screwed-up barnyard?"

"You got the good rooster—that's the most important thing. So you keep the rooster and get some hens that are on the rooster's trip. Slam dunk! Now we got some action!"

Moses burst out laughing. "Be something to see, all

right. Rooster out on the basketball court rousting all
them giddy hens."

"Dumb, huh?"

"Well . . ."

" 'Bout as dumb as some twelve-year-old cruisin'
Pittsburgh in a Rolls Royce that belongs to the best
round-ball player in the world."

"Yeah. 'Bout that dumb."

"But here we are." Tyrone smiled cockily.

"Here we are."

"So how dumb is this kid chauffeur?"

"Not too."

"And what we got to lose?"

"Not much."

"No more'n ten minutes, man. 'Cause we have an
important meeting with the big man—Mr. Tilson himself—in fifteen."

"Been wondering where we were headed."

"Now you know." Tyrone puffed up his chest.

"Now I know more than I wanted maybe." He
looked over at Tyrone, studying him, wary of the road
ahead and keeping a light foot on the accelerator,
but studying him all the same. "Tyrone, what made
you think I'd go for this?"

"Easy. Pisces always respond to a challenge."

"Always?"

"Well, if Jupiter's lyin' right, and Neptune ain't messing around too much with it—they're the planets that
rule Pisces, like I said."

"And you read 'em?"

"Lyin' just fine. Besides," Tyrone glanced down,
"Pisces rules the feet, and you handlin' the gas just
fine."

They laughed together.

3

The muscular masseur worked his hands over the man's soft back, moving from the waistline up toward the shoulderblades.

"Eeee!" the man sang, "that tickles. Stop!"

The masseur stopped.

"Harder."

The masseur frowned, flexed his heavy shoulders and large, square hands, and dug in. Now he plunged his thumbs deep into the muscles and flab, pressing to the bones.

"Aaargh! Mmmm, that's better. Keep doing that. Good."

The man was Halsey Tilson, who was fifty and had small shoulders, a large head, and a round, mobile face. His head was cocked up on his hands and he was reading the sports section of the *Gazette* propped on an easel in front of the massage table.

The headline read:

"PYTHONS' COACH & TEAM WALK;
'NOT WORRIED,' SAYS TILSON"

And under that was a picture that looked just like Halsey Tilson. But it was not. It was a picture of his brother, H. Sander Tilson, who was the owner of the Pythons.

" 'Not worried,' he says," Halsey muttered angrily to himself. "Oh no, not baby brother, not Daddy's favorite! Harder!"

The masseur dug his thumbs and fingers deeper into Halsey's back, the muscles on his own arms and hands rippling in the work.

"Always got to open his presents first. Dear Sandy was always first, poor baby was youngest. Never had to *work!* Just *me!* I had to work! I had to do everything! Then he gets the team. He's an idiot! Family fool!" He reached out, grabbed the page, wadded it into a ball, and hurled it against the wall. "Well, you can *start* worrying, Sander, you trust-fund retard!"

The masseur abandoned the back and began working on Halsey's toes, cracking the joints like walnuts.

"Oooh, good. More."

Halsey's legal counsel, Carvel Friesman, came tentatively into the room, his slicked-down gray hair parted in the middle, his shoulders in their permanent slouch, his mouth in its permanent sag. He clasped his hands behind his back.

Halsey looked over. "Baboon!"

"Sir?"

"My brother! Got the sense of a sawhorse, mind of a millipede, brains of a barnacle! He even *looks* like a baboon!"

"Ahem, well, he looks, in fact, quite like—um, erp—"

"Watches one game of basketball on the boob-tube" Halsey continued, "and suddenly he's all excited." He adopted a lisping, toddler's whine, " 'Oooh, super! Oooh, I wanna buy one! I wanna buy a team to play with, like my other toys! Where's my credit card?' The idiot!"

Friesman cleared his throat and bowed slightly. "Begging your pardon, sir, but your brother did inherit eighty million dollars and the family estate."

"Sure! Rub it in, Friesman," Halsey snarled, "and I'll rub you out! Harder!" His toes crackled like a campfire. "Yeah, he did, all right. Because I was making my own way and he couldn't take care of himself. Great idea. My brother is too addled to buy a morning paper, let alone work, so just give him everything and take care of him like he was in some *nursery* for the rest of his life!"

"I will admit, he did inherit quite a bit for a man of his—"

"Money isn't the issue here, shyster. It's the *name!*

The *slur* on the Tilson name. *My* name! Enough already!" He waved the masseur away and grabbed his robe. He swung his spindly, short legs off the table and sat up, pulling the robe around him. "Every place he goes, every time he opens his mouth, every time they put his picture in some magazine, it's an *insult* to the bloodline—which is *me!*"

Friesman bowed and nodded.

Halsey knotted the robe harshly around his paunch as if strangling somebody. *"I'm* the one carrying the load. *I'm* the one putting up with all the snickering at the Country Club! Just the other day," he glanced over at Friesman, "I'm about to tee off, and my partner says, 'Heard your brother ordered a big new batch of balloons with Python colors.' Can you imagine that? Hooked my shot right into the ball-wash! First game of the season, my brother makes me look like a sap!"

He dropped off the table and stomped into his office, Friesman dogging his heels quietly. "How much did that sucker Tucker cost us to move out?"

"Well, he still has a year to run, if we pay off his contract. But I don't think we have to worry about it. He'd do anything to embarrass Moses Guthrie."

"Guthrie! Aaargh!" Halsey grunted. "One's worse than the other. Like to see 'em all embarrassed. Music to my ears!" He paced back and forth. "Another thing. I want to re-open the investigation regarding my brother's mental competency."

"I don't think there are any new grounds for—"

"Moral turpitude! All his trains and balloons and what about that engineer's cap he wears?"

"Mr. Tilson, if I may. The courts have ruled against us three times."

"I can count, you legal bugle! That peckerwood's a raw nerve in me! The courts ruled wrong!" His face was like a beet. "So you put it in gear and come up with something or I'll ship you back where I found you—hustling whiplash cases on the Turnpike!"

"Yes sir, I'm always thinking."

"Thinking shminking! I wipe my nose with your kind of thinking. I want action! Claims! Suits! Writs!

Habeus Corpuses! Torts! Cross-exams! Tender offers! Get some law behind you. This ain't beanbag!"

"Um, anything particular you would suggest, sir?"

Halsey closed his eyes and thumped a fist on his desk. "Yes, yes, particular. Looka that crazy team. What more evidence do you need than that? He runs that team like a bunch of Lionel Little Leaguers. Complete schmoozle. Any judge could see it. He let the team go down the drain. I want him to go down with it. If you don't flush him, I'll flush you!"

"I'm sure we'll come up with something, sir."

Halsey cleared his throat and lowered his voice. "You understand, of course, I love my brother."

"Yes, sir, naturally."

"Naturally. I just want him put away."

"Yes, sir."

"I want him put away if you have to lop off his arms and legs and stuff him in a bottle of formaldehyde and put him on a shelf in the Mayo clinic like a jar of mayonnaise. Got that?"

"Yes, sir."

H. Sander Tilson's executive suite was like a miniature train yard. A model freight train snaked through a vinyl canyon and into a papier-mâché tunnel that cut through a clay mountain. Laid out on a double ping-pong table, the scene was an accurate representation of the Pittsburgh freight yards and the surrounding countryside.

The entire room was decorated in keeping with the railroad motif—lanterns, gold and steel rail spikes, a chrome steam whistle, various engineers' caps, crowbars, switch lights, and a variety of posters advertising "Tilson Freight Lines."

At the controls was H. Sander Tilson, smiling through his soft, baby-pink complexion, delight and energy showing in his eyes. He had on an expensive three-piece pin-striped suit and a blue-and-white striped engineer's cap.

Moses and Tyrone stood quietly behind him, hands behind their backs, waiting for a reaction to the presentation that Tyrone had just given him. The train whistle blew and Tilson clapped his hands. Moses and Tyrone glanced uncomfortably at each other.

"Whew! Marvelous! Just at the right time, before the crossing. Two longs, two shorts, one long. Perfect!" He watched the train hum around the track. "Very impressive, young man."

At the other side of the table stood Wally Cantrell, sniffing back bubbles.

Tilson waggled a hand at him. "Did you hear that, Wally?"

"Yes, sir. Good whistle, all right."

"No, no—well, yes, thank you. But I meant the boy. What a presentation, huh? And he didn't even use one of those silly blackboard graphs that you always use to make a point. Never did like blackboards. Reminds me of third grade, all those years there. The boy speaks well."

Tyrone beamed. Moses watched everything with a kind of pleased bemusement.

Tilson brought a second train in from a siding, heading it toward the first, and then executed a neat switching maneuver to avoid a collision. He clapped his hands. "Splendid! What a way to run a railroad!"

Assured that the trains were now running on separate routes, he turned to Moses and Tyrone. "Please, please, sit down. Have a train?"

Moses and Tyrone politely declined the trains but did sit down in the two director's chairs flanking Tilson.

Cantrell had been working himself up for some time. He was not one to push matters, worrying being more his style, but finally he could contain himself no longer. "Really, H.S., we have a major crisis to deal with, I mean, a player walkout and no coach . . . we can't afford to waste time. We've got to act fast or else the—"

"Fast? Fast. Hmmm." Tilson watched his trains and put a finger over his lips as if hushing everybody.

"Yes, sir, fast as we can or—"

Now Tilson did hush him with the finger over his lips. He turned to Tyrone. "Fast. What would be fast?

Let's see. Aha. What's the speed of light, my young friend?"

"Um . . ." Tyrone closed his eyes, pursed his lips, and said, "Through uniform transparent substances such as air, the speed of light is one-hundred-eighty-six-thousand miles per second." Then he opened his eyes to see Tilson nodding.

Tilson shut off his trains and went around behind his desk and sat down. He clasped his hands on the desk-top and leaned forward, looking first at Cantrell, whose nose wiggled like a rabbit's, then at Tyrone. He smiled. "Tell me more. I like your approach, young man. It's fresh. New. Got some youthful tang. Fun. Go on, tell me, let's have some more fun."

Tyrone glanced at Moses, who was looking at him expectantly, and then at Cantrell, who was snapping open another tiny envelope of antacids, then looked at Tilson squarely. "Well, sir, it's really quite simple. Um, well, it's a matter of basic compatibility."

"Yes, yes, yes." Tilson nodded happily. "I like words like that compatibility—basic, simple. It's my language you're talking. Yes indeed." He made a temple of his hands and leaned back, staring up at the ceiling and bringing the point of his hands up under his chin. "See, it was on my third birthday—or was it my fourth? Let's see. No, my fourth was the firetruck. So it must have been my third. Yes. On my third birthday I learned my first lesson in compatibility. Basic, simple. Lesson of a lifetime. Been my basic, simple, guiding lesson. See, my Auntie Eva gave me a set of building blocks. They had grooves on two sides, so they could fit together. Hmmm?"

He looked at his audience, all three of whom nodded dutifully.

"Yes. Well, one day one of the blocks was caught in a door and the grooves were smashed . . ." He paused briefly and seemed to choke a bit at the sad memory. "Yes, the grooves on that one block were destroyed. When I tried to use that in building things —like a house, I was good at that, you know—that one block didn't seem to fit. Didn't go with the others. Because it didn't have grooves, you see? Hmmm?"

They nodded.

"So that left me with a big decision. Yes indeed. And do you know what I did?"

They shook their heads.

Tilson fixed his questioning look on Cantrell, who finally realized he wanted an audible answer.

"No, sir," Cantrell said. "What did you do?"

"Ah! I got rid of it. Threw it out. Hurt to do it, but it was necessary. It was not, not—your word, Tyrone?"

"Compatible!"

"Exactly! Compatible. The block was okay for some things. I mean, I could have used it for something, but it was definitely *not* compatible with the other blocks. I'll have to use that word more often. Good word. Like to improve my vocabulary. Maybe get into more public speaking. They say if you use a word three times a day for three days in a row, it's yours. Hmmm?"

Everyone nodded.

Tilson smiled at the fond remembrance of his youthful decisiveness. He got up slowly and, seemingly lost in thought, went back to his trains and started them rolling.

Tyrone thought for a moment, then stepped over closer to him. "So you see, Mr. Tilson, the answer is in the cosmic complexities of the situation."

"Complexities?" Tilson snapped his head around and widened his eyes in concern.

"Well, simple, really. I mean," Tyrone continued, "the way so many things work together in a basic, simple way." He showed Moses a wisp of a smile.

"Ah. Simple. Good."

"For example," Tyrone went on, "do you remember the 1969 Mets? The baseball team? That surprised everybody by winning the championship?"

"Of course! How could I forget them? Follow sports all the time. Expert. I have doubles of Tug McGraw's baseball card. Want to swap?"

"So you know about Tug McGraw?" Tyrone asked.

"Certainly do! Was once offered all three Alous for one McGraw. Turned it down, of course."

"Do you know what McGraw was?"

"Relief pitcher!" Tilson beamed as if he had won a spelling bee.

"True. But he wasn't just an ordinary relief pitcher. He—"

"Not on your life! He was a *good* relief pticher!"

"Well, yes, yes he was. But my point is, he was a Virgo."

Cantrell, who had been shifting his feet and sputtering silently through all of this, snorted and wiped his nose. "Young man, what does that have to do with anything? We're talking *basketball* here, not baseball. And it doesn't matter what kind of pitcher McGraw was, since there's no spot for him in our lineup. So—"

"Oh hush up, Wally," Tilson said. "Tyrone didn't interrupt you when you were speaking. Proceed, Tyrone."

"Thank you. Well, in the fall of sixty-nine, the last weeks of the season before World Series time, there was a very unusual Saturn cycle that had a direct effect on McGraw's performance—down the stretch he was virtually unbeatable. Only once in twenty-eight years would Saturn have been in exactly that right position for him. That's how important it was."

Cantrell puffed out his lips, making small popping sounds with little bursts of breath between them. "Mr. Tilson. Please. We've *got* to deal with this problem."

"Oh yes."

"I mean, we've got chaos on the court. I think we should think about unloading the whole shebang."

"Unloading?" Tilson's attention was focused on a flatcar loaded with logs.

"Quite frankly, sir, *now* is the time to respond to your brother's last offer." He blinked, surprised at his own boldness. "That is, I think we—er, you—should consider it, at least. I'm quite sure your brother knows—"

"All he knows is how to make money. Halsey is an idiot. Any idiot can make money. Halsey does not laugh. A smart person is somebody who knows how to laugh. Or how to make others laugh. Halsey has never made me laugh once."

"Well, I really don't think this is a laughing matter."

"Ha-ha. Tee-hee. See? It is. It's fun. Tyrone's idea is fun."

Cantrell threw up his hands and stalked over to gaze out the window.

"Okay, you guys," Tilson said, smiling at Tyrone and Moses, "lemme think this over and get back to you."

They started to turn for the door.

"Hold it!" Tilson piloted a steam engine pulling a string of boxcars around to them, stopped it, and pushed a button that opened the boxcar doors. The cars were loaded with Animal Crackers and Oreos. "Wouldn't you like to take some cookies for the road?"

Moses controlled a chuckle. "No, sir. Thanks anyway. And thanks very much for your time."

"My pleasure, all mine. You're the star, aren't you? Moses Guthrie."

"Uh—"

"He sure is, Mr. Tilson," Tyrone piped up. "Just like I told you. It'll all revolve around him."

"Yes, yes, I understand that. But I mean, you are the star? The basic, simple fact is that you are the star?"

"Well . . ." He felt Tyrone's elbow jab him. "Yes."

"Good. Love to meet celebrities. Talk to you soon. Wally, would you escort these fine gentlemen to the door?"

The door was but a couple of steps away. Wally wiggled his nose. He sighed. Then he walked them to the door, opened it to usher them out, closed it, and came quickly back to the train table. "Well then, our problems are solved, I guess," he said with grouchy sarcasm unusual for him. "We'll just fire the scouts, get a couple of palm readers and some crystal balls—"

"Have an Oreo, Wally, and laugh a little at our good fortune. What a great story about the chicken and the rooster. That boy's got a fine future of his own. I can tell. I have a great sense of people. Do you realize that he's just saved me two million dollars in salaries?"

"I think you may be jumping to—"

"As a businessman, I must think about things like that. He's the kind of young man who belongs on the Tilson team!" They both watched the trains roll around. "Wally, do you remember the Tilson pledge?"

"Uh, well, yes," he cleared his throat uncomfortably, "yes I do."

Tilson had now guided five trains onto the tracks and was fascinated as he avoided one disaster after another by moving different levers with his pudgy fingers. "Let me hear it."

"Huh?" Wally gulped.

"Let me hear it! The pledge! It'll make us both feel good!"

Cantrell straightened his tie. "T—is for the Tilson team . . ."

"Louder! I can't hear you over the trains!"

"T—is for the Tilson team we play on . . ."

Tilson tooted the whistle.

"I—is for the ideas we write in crayon . . ."

Toot.

"L—is for the length of time we stay on . . ."

Toot.

"S—is for the shirts we wear of rayon . . ."

Toot.

"O—is for the accomplishments we work all day on . . ."

Toot.

"N—is for never-say-die no matter what goes on."

"Hurray!" Tilson tooted all the trains at once.

And so, a couple of days later, Tyrone went to work. Tilson had given him the go-ahead. "Spare no effort," Tilson had said. Moses, of course, still had some doubts, but he was secretly charmed by the idea. And anything was better than what had been going on with the team. He had no desire to become the laughing stock should this crazy idea backfire, but neither did he want things to go on as they were. So he supported Tyrone and helped with the details.

And the support of Moses was entirely crucial, naturally. Tyrone himself couldn't swing it alone. So when he put the word out—on radio and TV and in the newspapers, the name of Moses Guthrie was always included as a kind of validating testimonial.

The word that went out was a rather strange invitation to tryouts for a new Python team to be built around Moses Guthrie. The announcements specified only that the applicants "must have plenty of heart and desire" and that they have some basketball experience at any level at all, and that their birthdays fall between February 20 and March 20. The curious twist was the final line: "No players currently or previously employed by the N.B.A. need apply."

The announcements swept through Pittsburgh like wildfire.

On tryout day, which was a Sunday, a battered old Ford van with loudspeakers mounted on the top cruised through the downtown streets, headed in the general direction of the Civic Arena. The speakers were blaring a taped message: ". . . Cousy, Bill Russell, Jerry West, Willis Reed . . . great names from Basketball's past . . . pros, supermen. . . . But there's one name neglected among the greats . . . the Great Setshot . . . World's greatest free-throw artist . . ."

Driving the van was Horace Bufford, who called himself "Setshot." A small man of five-feet-four with short, scraggly blond hair and a cleft in his chin, Setshot had never played on any organized team exactly. What he did was shoot free throws. All his life.

On the sidewalk stood a much taller man, also blond but with longer hair. He had a glazed expression on his face and a set of headphones over his ears and a sign around his neck that said "Tryouts." In the headphones was music only he could hear. He smiled and hummed and held out his thumb to hitchhike.

Setshot pulled the van over, and the other man got in.

"Driftwood," was all the second man said, interrupting his humming.

"Setshot," Bufford said. But his own introduction went unheard. Driftwood just sat smiling and listening to his private music and staring straight ahead out the windshield. Setshot shrugged and steered the van on toward the arena.

In another part of town, inside the True Rock Gospel Baptist Church, the choir—all black and predominantly women—was belting out a rousing rendition of "Jesus, Won't You Walk with Me." They shook and quaked under their silvery gray silken robes.

Bracing the mahogany pulpit with his shovel-sized hands was the looming figure of the Righteous Reverend Grady Jackson. He was singing along with them, his voice booming over the congregation.

The Rev. Jackson was a tall, powerfully built man in his late forties, his hair a trim salt-and-pepper Afro parted in the middle. His size and demeanor commanded respect, and there was never any doubt in anybody's mind about his ability to command respect, whatever the situation. Sweeping his arms aloft, he inspired the entire church to join him in the spirited clapping of hands.

The packed church truly rocked.

At the end of the spiritual, the choir dramatically dimmed into one steadily held note—humming with the vitality of a power transformer—that provided the background for Rev. Jackson's virile baritone. He spread his arms, then brought them together and clasped his hands and bowed his head. "Brothers and sisters in Christ," he said, "let us lower our eyes, join our hands, and take this moment to rebound in—" He caught himself. "To *rejoice* in this communion with the Lord."

Shouts of "Amen" and "Praise His name" and "Yes, yes," came from the congregation as all eyes were lowered and all hands clasped. The Reverend stole a quick glance at his watch and continued.

"Lord, we welcome you here with us this morning, asking You to bless this house and all the free-throws —free *souls* gathered in Your magnificent presence. We know You gonna do right. We know You gonna help *us* do right . . ."

"Amen. . . . Say it, Reverend. . . . Yes, yes . . ."

" . . . And we bringin' our prayers to you on a

straight fast-break—er-uh, straight from breakfast . . ."

"Praise Jesus! . . .Tell it, Reverend . . ."

" . . . And we prayin' for You to shed Your light on this one-on-one—umma, this communion . . ."

"Oh yes! . . . Talkin' to You, Jesus. . . . Amen, Brother Reverend . . ."

Rev. Jackson peeked at his watch again, then leaned over toward the Deacon, who was standing near the pulpit with his head bowed. "Uh, Deacon Smith, will you kindly come and assist me in the prayer?"

"Wha?"

"We all talkin' to the Lord, Deacon. Time for you to give Him some words."

"Uh . . ." Deacon Smith edged up to the pulpit and raised his voice. "Yes, Lord." He glanced uncertainly up at Rev. Jackson, seeing him check his watch, and then tried to recapture the rhythm of the prayer. "We all in Your presence, Lord, night and day, all the time. And, and we ask You, Lord, for Your mighty forgiveness and guidance in all these times of toil and trouble and all that . . ."

Noting that all the eyes of the congregation were dutifully lowered, Rev. Jackson slipped out of the pulpit and down the steps to the aisle. Silent as a cat, he tiptoed past the rows of pews toward the door at the rear, completely unnoticed even by Deacon Smith, whose eyes were properly closed and who was concentrating on trying to find some more words.

At the rear of the church, an elderly parishioner who had fallen asleep suddenly awoke and opened his eyes. He saw Rev. Jackson sneaking by, holding his robe up from his ankles. And he saw that Rev. Jackson was wearing high-top basketball sneakers and knee-high white socks and no trousers.

At the same time, Deacon Smith ran out of inspiration and said loudly, "Amen!"

Now, at the door, Rev. Jackson stiffened at the silence. He sensed the eyes of the congregation turning toward him.

He looked back into the church and, with a flourish of his long arm, hollered, *"Hit it!"*

The always-prepared chorus immediately launched into "Rock of Ages."

Rev. Jackson dashed out of the church. Peeling off his robe, he sprinted down the front steps. By the time he reached his curbside Cadillac Coupe deVille, he was stripped down to a pair of vivid green satin basketball shorts and a black warm-up jacket across the back of which was stitched "FEED THE REVEREND."

He fired up the Caddy, and with the music billowing behind him, spun the wheels, screeching the car into a U-turn that aimed him for the Civic Arena.

Hundreds of cars were scattered around the Civic Arena parking lot, among them Setshot's van and Rev. Jackson's Cadillac. On the marquee over the entrance to the arena was the legend: PYTHON TRYOUTS— TODAY ONLY.

And under that, stretching far out into the parking lot, was a long line of hopefuls of all sizes and shapes and demeanor in all manner of attire, some carrying gym bags, some basketballs, some transistor radios, some lunch bags, and a few displayed copies of the team yearbook, *Python Portraits*. Most wore sneakers. A couple had on cowboy boots. One even wore football cleats. And one on stilts towered four feet above the rest.

From some of the radios in the line came the voice of the popular local disc jockey, "Jackhammer" Washington, whose Sunday show was on tape.

" . . . From QRAP, the rap station, this is the Jackhammer, the dapper rapper, comin' to you through the blue with soul meat for a Sunday treat. Yes, radio viewers, the ebony whippersnapper in the chocolate wrapper is on the case at a red-hot pace. We'll have three hours of the cream of the crop, the hits from the top. So just lay back and make contact. 'Fore we drop the stylus on B.B. King's new single, I just wanna tell you that the next time I see y'all, I won't be spinning sides, I'll be spinning balls . . ."

Finally the line moved inside, and within the confines of the gym the crowd seemed even more eccentric. The line broke up and people started milling around. Setshot pumped in imaginary free throws. Rev. Jackson paced and mumbled to himself, occasionally waving his arms benedictorily. A man in an Indian headdress tapped his feet rhythmically. Driftwood sat on a bench, weaving back and forth and smiling at the music in his headphones. A completely bald and silent black man in a basketball uniform continually spun a ball on one index finger then the other. A teen-ager in full motorcycle regalia—black leather jacket and black hat, studded boots, and gloves—stood glowering at anybody who passed. Behind him towered two gigantic women wearing leopard-skin trunks and tank shirts. Clomping back and forth was the man on stilts, his feet four feet off the floor, a radio clamped to his ear. In a particularly skillful move, he spread his legs to pass over a midget carrying a basketball and gobbling a hero sandwich.

Moses and Tyrone were in the locker room, watching this menagerie of potential players on closed-circuit TV.

"I declare, little buddy," Moses said, "my sign must be one of the weirdest in the universe."

"Well, *individuals,* you know—like artists, writers, poets, pianists—we bound to be dealing with special people. But don't forget the key to Pisces—support. Get 'em working right together, you got a tremendous force. Harness the imagination and individuality and you got a room full of greatness."

"What it looks like now is we got a room full of *crazy.*"

"Don't worry about how it looks, Moses. Trust me."

"Too late not to, little buddy." Moses chuckled. "Glad we don't have to work the tryouts ourselves."

"Brockington can handle it."

"Well, he's got the *spirit,* all right," Moses said, "but I don't know if he's got the *flesh* for it."

"He'll do fine. And Harry'll help him. Cantrell's up there in the stands, case anything goes *real w*rong."

"Yeah," Moses said, grinning thinly. "We got a rah,

rah assistant coach, a trainer and a fizzed-up general
manager."

Team trainer Harry Gunkle raised his bullhorn,
standing at attention as in his old Navy days. "Now
hear this! All right, you people, listen up!" His voice
rasped through the bullhorn. Some of the random
movement around the floor stopped. "You *will* secure
all this nonsense and you *will* form up in an orderly
three-rank. *Fall in!*"

There was no noticeable reaction from the noisy
circus. On the court sideline, three harried secretaries
from the Python front office tried to cope with the
confusing storm of applications, requests, and inter-
ruptions.

"What?" one of them said, cupping a hand behind
her ear to listen to a tall applicant wearing a wig, a
tight dress, and black mesh stockings. The secretary
was trying to hear over the chanting of a group of
Hare Krishnas clapping their tambourines and bouncing basketballs at the same time.

"I said I *ain't* no woman," the applicant said,
touching the wig. "It's just the way I *dress!* My private
life's none of your business. I'm here to play *ball,* so
to speak. So what you mean I ain't eligible?"

"Please, please, step aside . . ."

Sensing final rejection, she—or he—flounced off.

Harry managed at last to get some kind of order,
and to separate a few individuals from the mob to let
them show their stuff. First, he had each take the ball
and dribble to the basket for a simple lay-up. Some
bounced the ball off their feet, some missed everything
including the backboard. A few got the ball to the
hoop, and a few less than that put the ball in it. A
couple even did it well.

Then he had them take jump shots from the foul
line. The results were similar.

Then Harry loosened it up, telling each to just do
his thing.

Moses and Tyrone watched the closed-circuit monitor closely. But Moses did not match Tyrone's optimism.

"Well, my little man, looks like the planets are against us. I wouldn't have believed one single sign of the zodiac could cover so *much* garbage."

"Hey, it's lookin' bad right now," Tyrone said brightly, "but don't worry. The talent's out there. I can *feel* it!"

"If what you feel could be real. I guess only time will tell."

"And tell it *right!* The stars are with us, Moses— believe it! You gotta *believe,* especially with Pisces. That's part of the support thing."

"Yeah."

"And believe me, I'm gonna check it out for you with a first-hand look." He started for the door.

"I might as well come with you."

"Nope. You stay here. Get your vibes right first, Moses. Otherwise you'll have a bad effect on what happens out there. Psyche yourself up, think *positive!*"

"Yeah." Moses watched him leave, then turned back to the monitor and sighed.

On the court, the bizarre show continued. Waiting his turn on the sidelines stood a stern-looking man wearing a white Arab headdress secured by a woven rope around his head and draped down his back. He had signed in as Jamaal Truth, and was attended by a quartet of veiled Muslim women, each holding a ball on her lap as if it were a basket of wares in the Casbah. Cross-legged on the floor nearby sat Driftwood, wearing his stereo headphones and doing deep-breathing exercises.

As man after man went through his demonstration of skills, Wally Cantrell, in the stands, went through a series of Bromo-Seltzers. A row of cups filled with soda spread across the seat next to him, and he emptied one after the other. "Don't lose your grip, Wally," he muttered to himself as he stared at the performances below. "Things could be worse. Couldn't they?"

Suddenly he was brought bolt upright by a piercing war cry from the court.

A whooping Indian warrior in full battle dress and headfeathers rocketed onto the court riding a skateboard, wielding a basketball in one hand like a toma-hawk. He slalomed across the floor, scattering the other contestants, and zeroed in on the basket. He executed a precise kick-stop off the board, spun, and threw up a fine, successful hook shot.

When it swished through the basket, cheers went up in various languages, styles, and tones. A pair of twins, Kenny and Benny Rae, applauded the feat.

"Hey man," Benny said, nodding to his brother, "not bad."

"For an Indian!" he and Kenny finished off in uni-son, which they often did, cracking each other up. They slapped palms.

The Indian trotted over and stood before them, proudly, with great dignity. "Me Winston Running Hawk. Redman supreme. Warrior with mean hook shot and court savvy to boot." And then winking, he slapped palms with the twins, saying in a normal voice, "My calling card."

Kenny and Benny looked down at their palms, each of which held an Indian-head nickel. They grinned at Running Hawk. "Double-trouble!" they said together.

4

The continuing tryouts did not assuage Wally Cantrell's discouragement. He put down his soda cup and picked up the bull horn beside him. "Brockington," his voice boomed out over the court.

But there were so many dancing feet and bouncing balls and yells and whoops and moans and radios that Brockington didn't hear. He was then occupied chasing a fancy-dribbling Hispanic boy, trying to get his attention. " . . . I'm not trying to pressure you, honest! You can call your agent if you want to. But I just want to sign you up! You're a potential great asset to this team—great ball-handler, lots of spirit, will to win, drive, and ambition!"

The boy dribbled away, seemingly intent only on showing off to everybody.

"Please, please," Brockington begged, "think big! Great future! Python uniform! Home-town crowd roaring! Success! Pleasure! Team! . . ."

"Brockington!"

He stopped and looked around, searching the dome for the voice, while the kid dribbled to the door.

"Brockington!"

"Uh, um . . ." He saw Cantrell in the stands, but made a final move to go after the boy. "Wait!"

"Brockington! Get up here!" the voice boomed.

"Uh . . ." The boy had gone. Brockington's shoulders sagged. "Yes, sir." He trotted over to the stands and up the steps to the general manager. "You called for me?"

"Yes, if I may be so honored by a moment of your time."

"At your service, Mr. Cantrell," the assistant coach said seriously.

Cantrell sighed and indicated for Brockington to take a seat next to him.

Brockington sat stiffly, expecting the worst.

"Now then," Cantrell began, "correct me if I'm wrong, but you're aware of all the changes going on in the organization lately?"

Brockington's eyes opened wide and his voice trembled. "Oh yes, sir. But please believe me when I say that I'm sticking in, sir. I'm not with those quitters from before. I'm organization all the way. I never was part of that, not at all. My feeling is that when the going gets tough—"

"Fine, fine." Cantrell cut him off. "Now there's another change that Mr. Tilson and I wish to inform you of—effective immediately."

"Oh no, sir," Brockington was filled with fright, "not *me*. No need for that. I've been loyal. I'm trying hard. I'm really trying to do my job, motivate the team, always studying strategy—I'm even willing to go on the road and scout our opponents if necessary, if you'd like. I love this organization more than anything, and I beg you not to—"

"Effective immediately . . ."

"No . . ."

"Yeah. Here it is, right between the eyes."

Brockington closed his moist eyes.

"We've decided to name *you* head coach."

Brockington's eyes popped open, staring.

"Effective, as I said, right now, right here, today. The new head coach of the Pythons."

"Huh?"

Cantrell put an arm around Brockington's quivering shoulders like a scoutmaster. "I trust it's a job you can handle?"

At first the transformation in Brockington was gradual. His eyes dried, his shoulders stopped shaking, his chest stopped heaving. Then the change became abrupt and dramatic. His hands became fists, his jaw and chest stuck out, his eyes burned with fierce determination, his voice became as assertive as General Patton's. "Yes, sir! I've waited a lifetime for this kind of challenge. Am I ready? Well I *guess!* Can I do it? Yes, yes, *yes!*" He shook his head and grinned. "Boy oh boy! What a day! Head coach!" He swung a fist through the air, almost batting Cantrell's cup out of his hands. "Hot dog!"

Cantrell cleared his throat calmly. "Then you're confident you can work with all this . . . talent?"

"*Can* I! I'm telling you, Wally, as a coach I can see things out there on the court no one else can see. Little things. Things only a head coach can spot. Wow! Talk about a perfect opportunity for the right man!"

"Well, I do hope you're—"

"Vision's the operative word here, Wally." Brockington squared his jaw and looked stern, grabbing Cantrell's knee harshly, causing the general manager to jump. "There's a lot of raw potential out there I can whip into shape. I mean a *lot!*"

"Well then," Cantrell plucked Brockington's hand from his knee, "just go ahead and whip on, boy. Whip a lot. It's all yours, the whole shebang."

Brockington sprang to his feet, waving his fists. "I'll drive them, Wally! I'll inspire them! I'll make 'em work! I'll mold 'em into a fighting team! I'll make the substitutions and call the time-outs! I'll do *everything!* You can tell Mr. Tilson I'm going to deliver him a *winner!*"

This time when he swung his fist he *did* knock Cantrell's cup flying, soda splattering the general manager's face and blue suit.

"Uh, sorry, I'll—"

"Just go away and be the coach."

"Right!" Brockington flew down the steps and onto the court.

Through the rest of the afternoon, Brockington, assisted by Harry and an occasional word from Tyrone and a message from Moses in the locker room, had culled a team of those least likely to fail from the entire mob of those most likely to fail. Or, as Brockington saw them, "the best of a good lot."

Among the group assembled on the first two rows of the stands were Setshot, Rev. Jackson, Driftwood, Truth, Jackhammer, Benny and Kenny, and Running Hawk. Moses and Tyrone sat off to one side, Moses chewing his lower lip anxiously, Tyrone gazing happily into the air. Brockington paced in front of the team. Harry paced beside him, taking the roll.

Each of the players was chosen for having demonstrated a specially successful—if not talented—style. Setshot had stood at the free-throw line tossing in swishers interminably until asked to stop. Rev. Jackson had shown a special ability to move around the backcourt like he moved around the pulpit, directing and inspiring and occasionally taking the ball to the hoop himself for an impressive dunk shot. Driftwood, never removing his headphones, seemed to be a steadying influence on the group, and he seemed to have real talent. Jamaal Truth had a blazing intensity and a speed to match. Jackhammer, the disc jockey, was loose and slick, smartly rhythmic in his moves, and was a smart passer—when not prying at his Afro with his comb. Benny and Kenny, the identical twins, were so attuned to each other that they were able to uncannily anticipate each other's picks, passes, and cuts to the basket as long as they both were on the floor. And Running Hawk had a running hook shot just like he said, with the ability to fend off the defenseman deftly with his left arm while looping up the hook with his right, and applying just the right arc and reverse spin to bank it dependably off the board and into the net.

Whether all this added up to a professional basketball team was a matter still of great doubt, at least to Moses. But he had put his chips on Tyrone, and he let them ride there. He knew what he himself could do. And while he might have dismissed all this as nonsense in the beginning, he was impressed that it had actually come this far: there had been tryouts and selections and here sat a group of men with a special flavor to their game just odd enough to allow Moses to go with it—for curiosity if nothing else. Now as before, there was nothing to lose.

Harry held up his clipboard. "When I call your name, stand up so the coach can have a good look at you and associate you with your monicker." He ran his pencil down the board. "Jackhammer Washington?"

Jackhammer stood up, snapping his fingers.

"Okay, Washington, what do people call you in real life?"

"Real life? Don't give me strife. Jackhammer's the name, and it's always the same."

"Terrific. Just remind me to tape your mouth when I do your ankles."

"Cool it, Harry," Brockington said with his new toughness. "I'll handle the personnel."

"Yeah," Jackhammer went on, snapping his fingers and doing a little jive step, "if you was wise, white-eyes, you'd clam enough to realize Jackhammer will put you to the test, and show you which dude can rap the best!"

There was applause and muttered approval from his new teammates as Jackhammer passed down the line slapping palms.

"Enough," Harry said, again looking at his board. "Bufford. Horace Bufford."

He rose as Jackhammer sat. "I'd prefer it if you'd call me Setshot."

"It's your dime, Bufford—or Setshot or whatever. Just stand up and let the coach get a look at you."

"I am standing."

There were some titters as Harry now noticed how short Setshot really was. "Okay, Setshot. We'll do something. Maybe get you risers for your sneakers—or something."

"Harry." Brockington was stern.

"Okay. Heaney. Joseph Heaney—The Third."

Setshot nudged Driftwood, who rose and looked around, a faint hum audible from his headphones. He pulled off the phones and smiled.

"Just call me Driftwood," he said.

Brockington eyed him, then walked over, waggling a finger at him, narrowing his eyes. "You. Heaney. I seem to remember something. Weren't you, let's see . . . St. Bonaventure?"

"I think so."

"Top scorer and rebounder in 1969?"

"Something like that." Driftwood's smile remained.

"Right! Knew I remembered you! I'm an expert on stuff like that." Brockington nodded briskly and looked the player up and down, taking in his height and lean, hard muscles. "Where'd you disappear to, son? There were ten teams ready to sign you on the spot. You disappeared. Right?"

"Yeah." He shrugged. "I was protesting the draft, you know?"

Brockington stiffened, puffed up his chest, and pushed out his lips like a belligerent commander. "The draft! You ran from the war!"

"Nope," he smiled, "I *went* to the war, joined up. I was running from the *basketball* draft. Those people were like animals, jackals, hyenas, buzzards. And I wasn't a carcass or a lemming, so I—"

"Okay, okay. Harry?"

Harry resumed. "Next, Bullet Baines."

Bullet stood, grinning silently, the lights glistening off his bald head. He spun a basketball on his index finger.

"You're Baines?"

Bullet grinned and nodded, deftly switching the spinning ball from one index finger to the other.

"Well, don't you have anything to say for yourself?"

Bullet shook his head, passing the spinning ball between his legs.

"Okay, Bullet, nice talking to you. Next, Jamaal Truth."

Jamaal stood, swishing his headwrap back over his shoulder and glancing up into the seats where his entourage of veiled women now sat. Then he fixed his icy stare on Harry.

"Truth," Harry said, "what kind of name is Jamaal Truth?"

Jamaal glared at him. "A free man's name, honky.

I left my *slave* name in the slammer." His voice was as cold as his look, and as precise. "I see it all as a struggle for the consciousness to grow. It's my karma to go through the changes I've seen. I've been to the joint, I've been on the streets. I know where the truth is. And this Truth is now with the Pythons."

Cautious mumbles of approval came from the rest of the team, everybody a bit intimidated by his assertion of inner strength. Only Jackhammer dared to stand up and slap palms with him.

"Right on, brother," Jackhammer said, "from one to another."

"Amen," said Rev. Jackson, fingering the small gold cross dangling from a chain around his neck.

Harry sighed. "Okay, here I have two names on one line—Kenny and Benny Rae. One of those an alias?"

The twins rose together. Their Afros were trimmed short, and they wore matching basketball outfits.

"Two of you?" Harry tapped his pencil on his board as he studied them. "There ain't been a pair like this since Noah's ark. How are we supposed to tell you apart?"

Benny and Kenny raised their eyebrows innocently. "Us?" they asked in unison. "What do you mean?"

All the players laughed, including Moses.

Brockington raised his hand. "We'll use some kind of color coding. Don't worry about it, Harry. Tackle big problems first, the small ones fall into place."

Harry checked the clipboard. "Okay, big ones first. Winston Running Hawk?"

The Indian rose majestically.

Harry couldn't resist. "Tell me, Tonto—just between you and me—are you planning a little ticket-scalping on the side?"

Before Brockington could caution Harry, Running Hawk answered.

"With a face like yours, paleface, you should take a tip from the Lone Ranger and wear a mask."

Harry's face flushed as he opened his mouth.

"Harry."

"Yeah, Coach, okay."

But even Brockington was getting uneasy about the

array of characters before him. He rubbed his hands
together roughly to try to regain the proper composure
and positive attitude. "We got it, we got it. Everything's fine. Gonna put everything together. Winners.
Go ahead, Harry."

"Okay. Last one. The Righteous Reverend Grady
Jackson."

Jackson rose slowly and passed his gaze along the
other players and onto Brockington and Harry. "Gentlemen, it isn't every day that an ordinary minister
gets the opportunity to play for a fine coach like our
Mr. Brockington and be united with an equally inspiring and inspired congregation like ourselves. The
eyes of Him are upon us. I believe a few seconds of
silent devotion are in order."

He bowed his head and clasped his hands. His usual
leadership asserted itself, and everybody did the same.

"Works every time," the reverend mumbled.

When Brockington peeked up, everybody was watching him. "Ah, yes." He rubbed his hands together
again and began to pace. "Yes indeed. Fine words.
Fine sentiments. Brought us together. Yup." He
paced for a few seconds, getting his thoughts plotted.
Then he stopped and held up his left hand, spreading
the fingers. "See this, gentlemen?" He pointed to his
fingers with his other hand. "Five fingers. Got it? And
this . . ." He clenched his right hand. ". . . a fist,
See the difference? We'll go over it again. Five fingers,"
he held them up, "a fist. Separate fingers on the one
hand, together on the other."

He scanned the faces for signs of impact of the
statement. "Five fingers are five loose ends." He
waggled the tips of the fingers to demonstrate. "One
fist is power." He smacked his right fist into his left
palm. "We have a choice, gentlemen, a choice . . ."

"I pick Moses," came a voice.

Brockington ignored it. "We can either play it like
five fingers, or we can play it like a team. One is loose
ends, one is power. And I don't have to tell you men,
no man ever got knocked out by a finger."

Brockington resumed pacing, rubbing his hands together—so dry now from rubbing that they squeaked.

He was pleased with how things were going. These were moments he had dreamed of—addressing his own team—and he was pleased with his fluency. "Now, Harry," he turned to the trainer and held out his hand, " a piece of chalk."

Harry scrounged through his black trainer's bag and came up empty.

"Well, get the blackboard, at least."

Harry scampered down the court to the board, which was on a wheeled tripod, and started to shove it toward the team.

Running Hawk was eyeing Bullet, and suddenly called, "Coach!"

Brockington looked over, and Running Hawk pointed to Bullet, who rose, holding out both fists.

"Right," Brockington said, nodding with satisfaction. "Five fingers, fist. Glad you caught the idea."

Bullet never altered his smile, but with some quick sleight-of-hand moves reached forward and produced a piece of chalk from behind Brockington's ear. Then he sat down. Running Hawk proudly rubbed Bullet's bald head.

Brockington was momentarily taken aback, but struggled to regain his poise and control and take the bit of magic as a matter of course. "I like that, Bullet—always prepared. Good." He tossed the chalk in his hand and looked at his team. "We take on Detroit in five days—the league has given us that much time to reorganize the franchise. That isn't a lot of time, but I'm sure you're up to the task."

As Harry wheeled up the blackboard and Brockington turned to it, Tyrone nudged Moses and whispered, "What do you think so far?"

"Looks like the Gong Show—but," he added quickly, "I'm with it, right with it. We'll give it what we got."

Brockington studied the blackboard for a moment, then began to write with pride the phrases as he enunciated them.

"We have to . . ."

"Knock heads," Truth said barely audibly.

" . . . pull together!" Brockington looked soberly at the players.

"What I said," Truth mumbled.

"Now." The coach returned to the board. "We're going to do what's necessary to get the job done. You know what that means?"

"Play ball," Benny and Kenny said together.

"Pray," said Rev. Jackson.

"It means . . ." he wrote again as he spoke, "when the going . . . gets tough . . . the tough . . . get going!" He slapped the chalk down in the tray. He eyed the players with as close to an inspiring and commanding snarl as he could muster, rubbing his hands together. "Now let's get out on that court and shape up! Moses, take 'em out!"

The players got up, sort of cheering but emitting something more resembling a relieved sigh.

Moses led them out and tried to organize them into a weave drill, two lines of players facing each other from opposite sides of the court, each player from one line passing the ball off to one coming from the other direction. But everybody quickly went into his own specialty—Setshot positioning himself at the free-throw line, Running Hawk throwing up hooks, Bullet spinning the ball on his fingers and between his legs and around his head—and so on.

Moses looked wearily over at Tyrone.

Tyrone smiled and gave him the thumbs-up. "Support!"

Halsey Tilson sat at his desk, his back to a new team photograph on the wall. He held the newspaper up in front of him, reading closely. Behind the newspaper sat Friesman, fidgeting, swinging one leg across the other, looking at the ceiling, the floor, his hands.

"Listen to this," Halsey said. " 'The circus came to town yesterday in the form of tryouts for the new edition of the pathetic Pittsburgh Pythons. Barring any N.B.A. players from the selection process, the Pythons seem to be intent on designing a team that will be, to put it kindly, eccentric. That spirit might be said to reflect the attitude of the owner. Eccentric' . . ."

Halsey peeped over the top of the paper at Friesman. "Did you get that? Eccentric?"

Friesman nodded, unsure whether he was to be pleased or displeased by the word. But when he saw Halsey grinning, he grinned, too.

"Yeah. My brother. The Eccentric." He returned to his reading aloud. " 'Eccentric H. Sander Tilson, owner of the Pythons, who haven't had a winning season since their founding, claimed that these tryouts, in addition to filling the need to replace the squad that resigned almost en masse after the first half of their recent debacle against Boston, also served, as he put it, "as a dream come true for the many hopefuls who showed up yesterday." Whether dream or nightmare remains to be seen. It will be interesting to see what happens when everybody wakes up. And that should be when the Pythons host Detroit on Friday.' "

Halsey stopped reading, almost gagging on the final lines. He folded the paper and held it up. "How many of these do they sell?"

"About two-hundred thousand," Friesman said.

"Well, that means there are two-hundred thousand copies of *this*," he waved the paper, "floating around Pittsburgh." He smiled wickedly. "And every reader is a potential witness."

On Friday night everybody but Setshot was in the locker room, all dressed in their Python uniforms, ready for court action. Moses, as usual, sat a bit apart from the rest, turning a ball slowly in his hands, concentrating on the upcoming game.

But his concentration was not as complete as usual. Ordinarily he knew all the players and their abilities and their roles and matchups against the competition, so he could train his mind only on his own responsibilities. But here, he knew virtually nothing about everybody and what they could or would do in a game situation. He had tried to retain Tyrone's optimism, and to a degree had been successful—he was vaguely optimistic in a hazy kind of way. But there was no ignoring that the new crew that was to be the team operating around him was the strangest and least promising group of players with which he had ever been associated.

So while he was concentrating on his own game, he was concentrating as well on keeping Tyrone's mystical optimism in his mind, optimism based on the very strangeness of the players whom outsiders might see as hopelessly inept.

In the center of the room, Rev. Jackson was taking on Benny and Kenny Rae in a poker game. They were playing for nickels. Originally the game had included one more player—Running Hawk. Rev. Jackson now had a stack of Indian-head nickels in front of him. They all studied their hands.

Rev. Jackson tilted his face upward. "Lord, forgive me for what I'm about to do." He turned to Benny. "Now, I'm going to tell you what you're holding. You have a straight." He turned to Kenny. "And you have a full house."

The twins glanced at each other but did not otherwise react.

"But I . . ." Jackson spread his cards on the table, "have a straight flush, seven to jack." He smiled as they tossed down their cards, which were just the hands he had predicted. He raked in their nickels. "See, there was this card shark in my neighborhood. A deacon in the church, he was . . ."

Jackhammer came strutting out of the shower room, snapping his fingers. "Here's the Jackhammer, the old word-jammer, gettin' set for the first game where I'll stake my claim as the cat with the baddest moves and looks in the Python record books." Tugging his comb through his Afro, he sashayed past the cardplayers toward Bullet, who was sitting on a bench smiling like Harpo Marx.

Tyrone moved through, passing out orange slices. When he came to Bullet, Bullet moved his hands in a blur and produced an orange slice from the top of Tyrone's head. He handed it to Jackhammer, who slapped palms with him, shoved the slice into his mouth, and proceeded to his locker.

Truth and Driftwood sat next to each other. Truth had on his flowing Arab headwrap. Driftwood was in his headphones.

"I am descended from kings, man," Truth said to the unhearing Driftwood. "I traced my ancestors back to the Moors. I am the last of a long, long line of sheiks and pashas and a lot of other pooh bahs."

Harry came out of his trainer's room and stopped by the pair. "Hey, Truth, you can't wear that head thing out there."

"Why not?" Truth asked.

"It's against regulations."

Truth gave him a cold stare. "You better check on that."

Harry thought for a moment. "I don't know for sure. Maybe it ain't." He looked at Driftwood. "But I'm pretty sure you can't wear headphones. Hey, Driftwood, I'm talking to you."

Driftwood smiled up at him and slid the headphones away from his ears. "Sure, Harry, anything you say."

"You didn't hear what I said."

"Right." Driftwood replaced the headphones.

Harry walked away, and Truth resumed his monologue.

"My family tree extends into the fertile soil of the Nile, and past that even."

Driftwood nodded, in time to the music he was privately hearing in his transistorized headphones. "Outta sight."

Setshot entered the locker room, dressed in his warm-up suit, his face perspiring heavily. He had been outside the arena, practicing free throws against the wall. When he came through the door, he ducked as if afraid he'd hit the door jamb.

The twins looked up from their game.

"Hey, Setshot!" Kenny called.

"Why do you always duck when you come through the door?" Benny asked.

Setshot dribbled his ball awkwardly. "To play like a big man, you gotta think like a big man." He went to his locker and peeled off his steamy warm-up suit.

Harry shook his head and went back into the trainer's room. There he found Running Hawk immersed in the whirlpool, eyes closed in pleasure as he enjoyed the swirling water.

Harry scratched his head. "What're you doing?"

Running Hawk didn't open his eyes. "Taking a whirlpool bath, naturally."

Harry clapped a hand to his forehead. "You do that *after* the game."

"Oh."

Among the early arrivals at the arena were Mike and Michelle, both absorbed in their usual way. Mike scanned the soaring dome through his binoculars, Michelle gazed dreamily down into her issue of *Hollywood Star*.

"Like I been tellin' you, Michelle, you gotta go topside to really see it right." He panned the glasses around and sucked a long breath through his teeth. "Geez, she's a gorgeous piece of work."

"How can people say John Belushi's a sex symbol?" Michelle wrinkled up her nose at a picture of the actor.

Adjusting his focus, Mike zeroed in on the structural details of the dome. "Your average dumb toad wouldn't know it, but this whole roof's floating on silicone rollers."

"Silicone?"

"The rollers, yeah. To open the dome."

"Oh."

He frowned at her. "Why do you always gotta read when I'm talking to you?"

"Hmm?"

"Here." He thrust the binoculars at her. "Open your eyes and have a look at what I built."

She elbowed the glasses away. "My eyes *are* open and I already *seen* what you built. So build something else already." She turned back to her magazine. "I've had it with your dome, dear."

He took her chin in his hand and pulled her face around toward him. "Michelle, why do you refuse to improve your mind? It's really aggravating me."

She closed her eyes.

"You're surrounded by beauty here." He swept his

arm around. "I mean, why can't you relate to it? You know, you're a grown woman. You oughta have an appreciation for art."

"Do not harangue me." She opened her eyes slowly. "I've got my own mind."

"That's what worries me." He looked through the glasses.

"What do you mean by that?" she growled.

"Nothin'."

"Good. Do me a favor and zip your lip then. Thanks."

"Ain't love a treat," he muttered.

In the locker room, the players were dressed, ankles were taped, and they were pacing around ready to go.

Into the room came the new head coach, Brockington, wearing a red, white, and black checked blazer and wheeling the blackboard ahead of him. He pushed the board to the center of the room and circled it twice before stopping to write: "Rendezvous with Destiny!"

He motioned all the players to gather in front of him to look at the sentence. Brockington rubbed his hands together, rolling the chalk in his palms. Then he held up the chalk, showed it around, and put it down in the tray.

"I'm laying down the chalk," he said, "because there is no more time for diagrams. Tonight is the time for action. And action is a five-letter word spelled P-Y-T-H-O-N."

"Six," Truth said.

"Yes, six. Six-letter word. Pythons are action."

There were a few scattered "right on's!"

Brockington nodded around. He lowered his voice. "This is it, men. Detroit's out there tonight. Detroit rhymes with defense. They're big and they're fast. They're not here to have a friendly game of checkers. They are here to play basketball. But they play rough. They're out for blood—your blood."

He let that sink in. The players watched him casually.

"But they don't know what they're in for. The new

Pythons. New talent. New opportunities. New styles. New, uh, well, new coach." He looked modestly at his feet. "But you fellas right here will do the playing. And, um . . ." he was running out of inspiration.

Tyrone and his fellow ballboy Rudy had been standing at the rear. Now Tyrone edged between Moses and Bullet. "Coach?"

"Huh?" He looked up quickly. "What do you want?"

"Would you mind if I said a couple words to the players?"

"About what? What do you want to say?" Brockington looked confused and doubtful. "I'm telling them everything."

Tyrone looked at Moses in appeal. Moses nodded discreetly.

"Say, Coach?"

"What, Moses? You wanna talk to them, too?"

"Uh, no, just that, you know that guy from *Sports Illustrated,* that guy who was doing a story on all the coaching changes around the N.B.A.?"

"No. Oh, sure, of course. *Sports Illustrated.*"

"Well, that guy wants to include you in it. He was out near the bench. He said something about talking to you before the game."

"Me?" Brockington rubbed his hands together. "About talking to me?"

The other players caught on quickly, and nodded encouragement to the coach.

"Well, um, it's kind of—well, no rest for the weary. Guess I should go and talk to him. Good PR for the team, for the organization." He tried to slow down his words, to appear calm. "So, well, I'll go and give him a Python exclusive." He started out, then stopped and turned back. "One final reminder, guys—winners never quit, quitters never win."

They gave him some mild cheers of encouragement, and he left.

Rev. Jackson tapped Moses on the arm. "Hey, man, what's happenin'?"

"Better let Tyrone explain."

Tyrone stepped in front of the group. "Thanks, Mo-

ses." His eyes swept the faces of the players towering over him. "You guys are probably wondering why
a boy like me wants to talk to you. Well, I guess
some of this whole thing was my idea—not that I'm
specially brilliant or anything. But the fact is, well, I
gotta tell you guys something. The reason you were
picked, as you must've figured out by now, is 'cause
you're all born under the sign of Pisces . . ."

"The Fish!" Rev. Jackson put in, surprised he hadn't
thought of that before.

"Right. You cats are all Pisces, which was the sign
the sun was in when you were born. Now, guys like
me—Aries and a couple others—are fire-sign people.
Pisces and a couple others are water-sign people. And
those are the most emotional types. You cats are all
astrologically compatible. Now, the sign you're born
under doesn't mean you *have* to do anything. But you
Pisces got all the qualities to do fantastic things—together. I don't want to go into the whole zodiac business right now, but you guys working together can do
just about anything you set your minds to. You guys
could take on a whole army and win. It's 'cause the
cosmos—the whole universe—is on *your* side."

"Whoowee!" spouted Running Hawk, shaking his
headdress.

"Wait a minute," Truth said. "I'm not sure about
any of this."

There were some mutters of approval and disapprov-
al, some sounds of uncertainty.

Moses held up his hands. "Just listen, that's all."

They listened.

"I know none of this makes a whole lotta sense to
you right now," Tyrone went on. "But you wait and
see. It's not something you gotta *do*. It's a *feeling*.
When you get out on the floor, you'll feel it."

They listened more intently—relieved that nobody
had to do anything more special than ordinarily.

"You'll feel different. You'll feel like you're a piece
of something that's bigger than just you. You just gotta *believe*."

"Say it, brother!" Rev. Jackson chimed in.

"Remember, it's the chemistry of the cosmos you

gotta believe in. It's the Pisces combination that will make it work." He looked at them closely, then shyly lowered his eyes.

Moses came over and put an arm around him. "Don't worry about swallowing it all whole," he said to the team. "Let's go play some basketball."

For a moment the room was silent. Then they broke out with pre-game spirit.

"Let's go!"

"Hit the court!"

"Take it to the Pistons!"

And they filed out of the locker room and into the tunnel that would take them to the floor. Driftwood was wearing his headphones. Truth had on his Arab wrap. Jackhammer jammed his Afro comb into his hair and left it there. Setshot continually adjusted his wristbands—the precise position of which he believed contributed to his precise touch at the free-throw line.

5

It didn't hit them until they walked onto the court. There was Detroit, going through its warm-ups, swishing shots from all angles, big front-court men stuffing rebounds down into the net with powerful ease. And the crowd, larger than usual because of the unusual publicity and expectations of a crazy show, surrounded and intimidated them.

The Pythons bunched up and bumped into each other, all except Moses who, suddenly aware that they were actually going to play a professional basketball game, felt a little weak in the knees.

"Ladies and gentlemen," came the public-address announcement, "the new Pittsburgh Pythons!"

Moses nudged them forward and they headed for the ball rack at center court. They took balls, looked at each other, started a few of the drills and shots Moses had taught them in the last couple of days, and then they all reverted to type. Everybody went into his own thing—Running Hawk taking wild hooks, Setshot shooting "free throws" from wherever he happened to find a loose ball, Truth staring hostilely at the opposition while taking no warm-up at all, Jackhammer jabbing at his hair with his comb while dishing clever passes off this way and that where there was no one present to receive them. Only Moses looked like a basketball player, taking smooth jumpshots from outside, loosening up with driving, spinning moves to the hoop.

Chuckles began coming from the crowd. Gradually the Detroit players ceased their own warm-up and moved toward center court to wtach, elbowing each other gleefully.

High in the stands, Mike, hearing remarks from other spectators, tilted his binoculars down toward the court. "Hey, Michelle, just lookit those clowns down there, will ya!" Getting no response, he elbowed her in the ribs.

"Ouch! Hey!"

"Yeah, well when I tell ya to look at something, will ya look at something?"

"Maybe yes, maybe no. You don't have to beat me up."

"Just look down there."

She looked at the court. "So I'm lookin'. I ain't impressed. They look like a bunch of refugees."

"Yeah—from some mental institution. What a mess to bring into this place." He reached down beside him to pick up his can of beer, and something caught his eye under Michelle's chair. "Hey, Michelle, mind if I look at your seat?"

"Michael!" She looked at him coyly.

"Naw, naw, your *seat*. The seat you're sittin' on. So will ya stand up? I got work to do. This whole place is goin' to the dogs."

She grudgingly stood up. Mike flipped open his belt-hung tool kit and fished out a screwdriver as he knelt beside her seat. He busied himself tightening a screw that had worked loose and was sticking up. He pushed at her leg to move her farther out of the way.

She rolled her eyes. "Mike, maybe you'd better see a doctor. You're really getting weird. We're supposed to be at a basketball game."

"Can't play proper ball in a place that needs work." He tested the swinging seat mechanism and winced at its squeak. "Wish I had some three and one oil."

Ola and Brandy arrived at the game earlier than usual—before it actually began. They put down their portable tape player, looked at the court, and immediately began to giggle.

"Will you check that out?" Brandy squealed. "Where did they find these doofuses? Musta drug the river."

"That bald one's kinda cute," Ola said. "Gimme your program."

"Sure. Here. You always had a weakness for baldies."

Ola quickly flipped the pages. "Here he is. Bullet Baines. I like that name."

"Bullet! Wonder if that means he can shoot?"

"Well, it better. Don't look like they gonna be able to do nothin' else down there."

The courtside timekeeper hit the buzzer to end warm-ups. The teams gathered at their benches, then the starting fives ambled out to the center jump circle.

Rev. Jackson would start at center, Moses and Driftwood at the forward, and Setshot and Bullet at guard.

The Detroit players had a hard time getting set. They knew where they were supposed to line up, of course, and what they were supposed to do, but they were distracted by their opponents. They kept chuckling and elbowing each other.

"Hey, Moses," asked his opposing forward, "where'd you get these cats? Barnum and Bailey?"

"From the stars, man," Moses said.

The referee tossed the ball up, the Pistons' center Bob Lanier easily outleaped Jackson to tip the ball to his forward. But Moses anticipated it and lunged to knock it away.

Setshot picked it up, eyed the basket, then thought better of it and looked around. He passed up ahead to Driftwood, who quickly sent it to Bullet. Bullet spun the ball on his finger for a second, then tapped it away with his other hand to Rev. Jackson near the hoop.

Jackson raised the ball as if to shoot. "Amen." Lanier flew through the air to block the shot, but Jackson ducked him, then laid it up for the score. "Like I said, Amen."

Detroit's guards brought the ball back upcourt. The Pistons were still disorientated by the unorthodox style of the Pythons. Moses played his man tight to keep him from getting a pass. One guard tossed to the other, not even noticing Setshot standing in between. The ball bounced off Setshot's ear. He picked it up, dribbled unevenly over the center line, then stopped and gazed wistfully at the hoop.

He was forty feet away. While Detroit fell back for defense, Setshot steadied himself, pursed his lips, and lofted a high shot. It was perfect, never touching the rim as it swished through.

The crowd, like the Detroit team, not ready for any of this, reacted with hesitant cheers.

"All right!" Moses said, glancing over toward the bench at Tyrone.

Up in the high seats, Michelle bounced to her feet to cheer, stepping on Mike's hands.

"Hey, watch it!" He was on his hands and knees, moving from her chair to the next one. He tightened screws and made other adjustments there, and moved on. From seat to seat he scrambled, tightening, checking, testing, nodding approval at each completed repair. Many of the seats were empty. A popcorn-munching couple gaped with disbelief as he crawled in between their seats like a bear sniffing for berries.

"Don't take alarm, folks," Mike said. "Just pretend I'm not here. Working behind the scenes, that's my style." He continued down the row.

Bullet dribbled the ball upcourt, then passed off to Setshot. Setshot eyed the basket. His defensive man immediately crowded him to prevent a recurrence of the lucky long-distance shot. But Setshot passed instead to Moses.

Moses never even had to look at Bullet, who was cutting for the basket. He passed to him over his shoulder.

Bullet took the pass and left the floor, the ball spinning on his right index finger. When the defender leaped to block that, Bullet, in mid-air, switched the ball to his other index finger and laid it up—another score.

Now the Detroit team, embarrassed, began to bicker among themselves. "Stay with your man . . . don't go for those crazy fakes . . . settle down . . ."

Moses slapped palms with his teammates as they dropped back. All the Pythons were smiling—Driftwood and Bullet never did otherwise anyway.

Brockington tried to control his amazement. He didn't want it to show. A general should be somber, he told himself. He paced back and forth in front of the bench and wondered if he should call a time-out for some reason.

The game continued in the same odd fashion with which it began. Detroit was discombobulated, unable to organize effectively on either offense or defense against a team that seemed to have no rhyme, rhythm, or reason for being able to do what it was doing. The ball just seemed to end up in Python hands and thence in the Python basket. The Pythons seemed to have no recognizable strategy or to run any recognizable plays. The only exception was Moses, whose game came together as it hadn't since he entered the pros. He scored from everywhere, and especially from clever drives and soaring leaps around the basket. Playing as he was, he would have been unstoppable anywhere.

Brockington substituted now and then, for no particular reason and with no particular effect.

Detroit brought the ball upcourt against Moses, Running Hawk, Truth, Rev. Jackson, and Jackhammer. The inspired Pythons played tight defense. And Detroit was now pressing too hard. A forced pass into Lanier was batted loose by Jackson. Truth recovered and passed to Running Hawk.

Running Hawk stunned his defensive man with a wild war whoop, flashed by him, and sent up a hard hook shot that banked in.

Mike by now was all alone in the topmost tier, working on the seats. He paused in his repair rounds to watch a bit of the action, and got caught up in it like everybody else—the whole crowd was now cheering. He waved his screwdriver. "Way to go, Pythons!" he yelled.

When the buzzer signaled the end of the first half, the Pythons led, 56–45.

As the teams left for their locker rooms, the crowd cheered for the Pythons like they hadn't in years.

The atmosphere of the Detroit locker room was one of dismay, eased somewhat by disbelief—that is, however badly things had been going for them, the players did not believe that this kind of wacky game would go on for another half.

"Who *are* those cats?" Lanier asked, slapping a towel across his back. "They ain't supposed to play no ball like this."

"Ain't *nobody* supposed to play ball like this," somebody called. "This ain't real *ball*."

"Guthrie's killing us, man," said somebody else. "Ain't never seen him so quick and his eye so good. We gotta double up on him."

"And that little cat," said a guard, "that little white dude that took that long shot—where'd they get a midget like that? He don't do nothin' like anybody's supposed to do. He just squirts around where you can't find him. Then he puts that shot up like it's wired to the hoop."

"And that *baldy* out there. Ain't there a rule about spinning the ball like that? Interrupted dribble or something?"

"And that weird Indian . . ."

"And that crazy Arab type staring me down . . ."

"And that guy with the earphones, I remember him from somewhere . . ."

"And that center they got. How you s'posed to play when some dude's prayin' in your ear all the time?"

The mood of the Python locker room was entirely different. Except for Moses, who sat calmly sucking on orange slices, the players were exhausted. A full half of professional basketball was nothing like anything any of them were used to. They were buoyed by their performance and the score, but they didn't talk for a while, until their chests stopped heaving.

Coach Brockington strode around patting people on the head, tapping their shoulders, holding up a proud fist. "Way to go, fellas," he kept repeating. After a while, he expanded. "Create the breaks, as they say, keep doing that. You create your own breaks. And the breaks are coming our way because you're creating them." He wheeled out the blackboard and wrote on it as he said: "Persist and you'll succeed!"

"Amen," came from Rev. Jackson.

"We ain't stars," crooned Jackhammer, teasing his hair with his comb, "but we *got* the stars."

Moses winked at Tyrone.

Jackhammer's allusion was obscure to Brockington, who had not been privy to Tyrone's earlier discussion about their astrological sign and the significance of it. But Brockington didn't care. Things were going well, and he attributed much of that to his sensitive timing in making substitutions and calling time-outs. "The second half will be ours because Detroit doesn't know what's going on out there," he said with unwitting accuracy.

Upon returning to the court, the Pythons were treated to a rousing ovation. Rising above the general din came Ola's piercing voice, "Bullet, Bullet, Bullet!"

They gathered around the bench, slapping each other's backs and behinds. Brockington, carrying a clipboard on which he had written, "TIME-OUT," walked among them, rubbing his hands.

"Now guys," he said, "remember, the coach is just the coach. *You* guys are the players. Don't forget that."

When Ola and Brandy, jumping up and down on their seats, combined their voices to holler, "Bullet!" the sound finally reached Bullet himself. He turned to look up at them, flashed his smile, and from somewhere produced a plastic rose, which he waved at them.

Ola screamed in ecstacy and fainted into Brandy's arms.

"Oh, girl," Brandy sighed, "you just got no resistance at *all*."

Before the starting five went out, Tyrone leaned in among them. "You guys can't miss. The moon is in Neptune. Put your sign on the line!"

For a couple of minutes the teams went back and forth without a score. Then Bullet dazzled his man with a pass between his legs to Jackhammer who snapped it inside to Truth. Truth fixed his man with an icy stare, rooting him to the spot, and drove around him to lay it in.

Detroit missed their next shot, Moses took the rebound and passed upcourt to Jackhammer, who had been hanging back trying to catch his breath. He was all alone and scored the lay-up.

Detroit came down again. This time Jackhammer was on his man. He dove for a steal, and missed. The now-open man sent up a jumper, but it bounced off the front of the rim, coming far out to Truth. Truth tossed to Moses, who was already streaking. Moses, with his long strides, outran everybody, scoring with a showboat takeoff from the foul line and a backwards dunk.

The fans howled their approval. The effect on them was electric. Spectators dropped soda cups and choked on bites of hot dog; vendors, their eyes on the game, tripped over feet and sent their trays flying; programs were hurled into the air.

Detroit scored a couple of times, quieting everybody quickly. But then Running Hawk dropped one through and went into a war dance, bringing the crowd up once again.

At the start of the fourth quarter, the Pythons led, 91–63. By now, the mood of the Detroit players was that it was just one of those nights. So there was nothing significant about it. Teams have them all the time. The players wished somebody *else* might have had the off night against the ridiculous new Pythons in their first game, but professionals had to accept such nights as this in any case. It was a long season, and you couldn't let one game get to you.

And so the Pistons relaxed. And in so doing they began to play better. They scored four quick baskets. Whether the Pythons became disorganized or not was hard to tell, since organization was not one of their hallmarks, even in building the big lead. Brockington called a time-out and stomped around rallying the panting players with words about going the extra mile and hanging tough and running good plays.

Play resumed in Detroit's forecourt. A quick pass inside found a Piston open for a lay-up. But Driftwood, showing what had made him a standout years before in college, left his own man and came out of nowhere to swat the ball away.

Rev. Jackson grabbed it in one hand and passed up to Setshot. Setshot took a few cautious dribbles over the midcourt line, stopped, aimed, and threw up a tremendously long two-hander as he had done early in the game.

It came nowhere close to the basket. Setshot slapped his hands over his eyes. So he didn't see that Moses, always hustling, was down there under the ball when it came down. He took it like a pass and laid it in.

Detroit scored twice more. Bullet brought the ball upcourt and passed to Setshot, who was still thinking about his missed shot. He didn't want to shoot again under any circumstances. He called out the number "two," dimly remembering that there was a play of that designation. He gave the ball to Bullet, whom he figured might remember what the number two play was. Bullet didn't know either, and gave it to Moses. Setshot just tried to get out of everybody's way, so he went under the basket where there was nobody else. Moses passed in to him. It bounced off his head high into the air. Rev. Jackson leaped with Detroit's Lanier, and it went off both their fingertips into the net.

Detroit scored three more baskets. Brockington sent in Benny and Kenny.

The twins passed the ball back and forth, without looking at each other. Benny went for the basket, Kenny slipped a bounce pass through. Benny went up as if for a lay-up, but passed back to Kenny. Kenny dribbled toward the basket, and passed back to Benny. As the twenty-four second clock ran down, it seemed that those two were the only ones on the court, and neither would take the shot. But suddenly they broke for the basket shoulder to shoulder and both of them banked the ball home.

Michelle looked around for Mike, couldn't find him,

took his binoculars, aimed them at the court, and screamed, "Murder 'em, ya gorgeous brutes!"

The teams traded a few baskets, Moses now doing most of the scoring for the Pythons—most of everything, in fact. He brought the crowd to its feet with a court-length drive, a vision of coordination, speed, and grace. From the foul line he spun in mid-air, double-clutched, and slam-dunked in one smooth motion.

Other than the job by Moses, the Python scores were difficult to understand—except by Tyrone. That an off-balance running hook by Running Hawk bounced off the rim, went nearly to the dome, then fell cleanly back through the net, didn't surprise Tyrone. Nor did it surprise him when Jackhammer stood jawing in rhyme to a Piston, and the player knocked the ball savagely out of his hands, and the ball ricocheted among several hands and finally went through the hoop.

Tyrone knew the planets were right.

To the roaring delight of the fans—especially Ola and Brandy and Mike and Michelle and the men in wheelchairs at the end of the court (many of whom remembered when there was no such thing as basketball)—the final score stood at Pythons 112, Detroit 83.

When the horn blew to end the game, Tyrone leaped up among the other Pythons, waving his fists in the air. Brockington hopped up and down, stunned and unable to speak. Moses led the Pythons off, and was the first to slap palms with Tyrone.

By the next day, a lot of the happy shock had worn off, and the Pythons were not all that sure about what had happened or what it meant. They straggled out of the players' entrance at the arena, carrying their travel bags and headed for the team bus that would take them to Washington for their next game against the Bullets.

"The Lord was with us last night," Rev. Jackson said, "that's a fact. 'Cause nobody but him coulda pulled that off."

"Maybe it was a fluke, like they say," Setshot said.

"Can't be no fluke. Flukes don't come that big. Had to be the Lord or one of His Deacons."

"Fine with me," Setshot said.

"The Lord got Deacons?" Truth asked.

"The Lord got whatever he wants, " Jackson said.

They climbed aboard the bus and settled in.

Jackhammer strode up the aisle, slapping palms left and right. "Old Jackhammer's part of the load when we take this magic show on the road!"

"Dig it!" Benny and Kenny said together.

"My hook's gonna cook!" Running Hawk said.

"Hey!" Jackhammer gave him a look of mock annoyance. "*My* time for rhyme, without no Hawk talk!"

Toward the rear, Truth sat talking to Driftwood, who, of course, couldn't hear with his headphones on. "I was *on* last night, my cool self! It was just like the young brother, Tyrone, said. Maybe 'cause I got *roots*. Go way back, you know. Think I got some Piltdown blood in me."

"It was weird, man," Driftwood said, removing his headphones. "Did that really happen? Or was it a dream?"

"Bit a both. What you think, Bullet?"

Across the aisle, Bullet grinned, rubbed his head, and produced a cigarette, which he handed to Driftwood.

"Far out," Driftwood said, lighting up and putting his headphones back on.

Moses sat by himself in the back—not because he shunned or was shunned by the other players, but because he was engrossed in studying some papers on his lap. It was his astrological chart and forecast prepared and signed by Tyrone.

Tyrone wasn't traveling with the team. He wished he were, of course, but couldn't miss school. But now he wished he was with them more than ever because he felt it would be necessary to reinforce the astrology concept to them. And the day had gone by, then the evening, and he was dying to know how they did.

He was sitting on the floor, his eyes glued to the TV, watching the report by Murray Sports.

"The Pythons surprised everyone again tonight," Murray said, glancing down at his notes, "as they up-set Washington with some sharp shooting by Moses Guthrie and some complex and rather mysterious playmaking by his teammates . . ."

Tyrone yelped a cheer.

" . . . Guthrie scored forty-three points. Newcomer Setshot Bufford had twenty—most of those on free throws. Jamaal Truth had eighteen, and Jackhammer Washington twelve. Except for Guthrie's splendid dis-play of shots, most of the Python points came on un-orthodox maneuvers too complicated to go into here . . ."

Tyrone cheered again.

"Tyrone," Toby called from the kitchen, "what was the score?"

" . . . The new-look Pythons thus continue to amaze the basketball world . . ."

"Tyrone?"

". . . with a bunch of seeming misfits and weir-dos . . ."

Toby walked in, drying her hands. "What about the score?"

" . . . Oh," Murray said, as an afterthought, look-ing again at his notes, "the final score was Pythons 122, Washington 118."

Tyrone whooped and rolled around on the floor. "Get *down!*"

"Pretty close," Toby said.

"Don't matter! Pisces ain't picky about the margin, just the win!" He hopped up and hugged his sister.

She spun him around happily. She loved to share Tyrone's successes. They had always been close, and she had always seen to his welfare and been reward-ed by seeing him grow strong and intelligent and hon-est. She protected him through a series of foster homes, and then took him with her when she went out on her own—slipped away with him, actually, since techni-cally they belonged where the county put them. And they had been together and close ever since.

And for Tyrone, his sister was the most important person, the one to whom he took his problems, but also the one to whom he most enjoyed taking his news of satisfactions and progress.

She did not entirely share his trust in astrology, but certainly something had happened to turn the Pythons around. So they hugged each other and danced around the room, laughing.

The Pythons continued to win on their road trip, and the headlines of the local newspapers' sports pages reflected their amazing rise:

PYTHONS CRUSH CHICAGO; BULLS CALL IT "LUCK"

PITTSBURGH DOMINATES DENVER AS "MAGIC MOSES" SCORES 46

CINDERELLA TEAM TOPS SEATTLE

PYTHONS CONTINUE STREAK AS BOSTON FALLS BY 10

PYTHONS ANNIHILATE ATLANTA: DOES MOSES HAVE LUCKY STARS?

And with the wins the Pythons climbed quickly up in the standings. A play-off spot seemed actually within reach—something undreamed of just a few weeks before.

But then they lost twice. It wasn't just that they lost, they were blown out by Phoenix and New York. And it wasn't just that they lost badly, they had somehow come apart as a team, each of them reverting to the oddball individuality that they originally displayed at the tryouts. The teamwork was gone. They won their next game at Portland, which ended the roadtrip on an upbeat.

But Tyrone sensed trouble. He had to work fast. And he had to be lucky, too. But he had always been lucky. He had the energy and the will-to-win of the true Aries, and believed in making his own breaks, or at least taking advantage of them.

And one of the breaks that he trusted as a sign of luck and fate, and that he would now use to advantage was his fortuitous collision many days ago with the man carrying the sandwich board.

So, toting a sheaf of papers, Tyrone walked past the bookstore, scanning the delapidated storefronts beyond. And then he found it—the dingy doorway the man had entered after bumping into him, the door on which was roughly printed, "Mona's Astrological Temple."

He went in and made his way up the shadowy stairwell to the upper landing, which was lit by a solitary bare bulb. At the landing were three doors, two unmarked, and one with a hand-drawn, ornate sign that said,

---

MONA MONDIEU—ASTROLOGER
** Cash & Credit Cards Accepted **
NO CHECKS
****
DO COME IN! ! ! !

He smoothed his hair down, opened the door, which produced a sound of chimes somewhere inside, and stepped in.

With his first view of the room, he let out a low whistle. He had just entered what looked like a magic land. Illuminated by dozens of candles, the tiny room was wallpapered with heavenly charts, obscure diagrams, and renderings of the zodiac. The ceiling was covered by a mural of the zodiac done in the most complicated and intricate style he had ever seen. And around the room on small tables were astrological bric-a-brac, figurines of rams, archers, crabs, fish, and the like.

From beyond a beaded curtain came a melodic voice, "Be right with you!"

Tyrone nodded as if he could be seen, and walked slowly around the room studying the various items and displays. He paid special attention to a Day-Glo painting on velvet, labeled underneath, MONA MONDIEU, and showing an attractive face with penetrating eyes and full lips formed into a mysterious smile, surrounded by a cascade of curly brown hair to her shoulders. As he passed the curtain, he could hear the voice behind it.

". . . Being a double Scorpio, your problem is complicated. Don't worry about the late alimony to your first three wives, just concentrate on making your new bride happy. Your moon is *definitely* in the bedroom. Things will stabilize when your third house comes into conjunction. That'll be nine ninety-five, please."

Tyrone heard the scraping of chairs being slid back. He stepped away from the curtain and watched.

Through the bottom of the curtain came a middle-aged midget, his dark hair slicked down, his mustache pomaded. He nodded to Tyrone and said in confidential, Spanish-accented tones, "Take it from me, muchacho, walk *tall* and never get married. *Comprendes? Bueno.*"

"Uh, yes, sir."

The curtains swished open and Mona Mondieu poked her head through. "It's yes, *ma'am* in this parlor," she said teasingly, flashing a fan in front of her face.

"Oh. Yes, ma'am. I just meant . . ." He turned to indicate the midget, but the little man was gone. "Yes, ma'am."

Mona snapped her fan closed and smiled as she let the curtain fall behind her. She was dressed in black chiffon and lace, with a deep V-neck and several lockets dangling around her throat. "That's better. Now, young man, what can Mona do for you?"

"Well, uh, I'm Tyrone Millman. And, er, well, I got this term paper to do, about astrology, you know? And, um, I worked out some stuff, some charts, and I thought, well, maybe you would look at them, and maybe comment on them, you know. I mean, I will pay you for your time, if you want, if it's not too much. Just for school, you know?" He stuck out his hand and she took it gently, eyeing him.

"I usually get older men, but you're sorta cute, Tyrone. Glad to meet you." She gazed off. *"Aries."*

"Huh? How'd you know?"

She smiled enigmatically. "Because Mona knows, that's all. Aries is the Ram and I'm the astrologer.

You have all that Mars aspect in your voice, your tone, your bearing. Straightforward, direct, competitive —very Ram."

"Competitive?" He was flattered and impressed.

"Yes. Aren't you?"

"Well, I guess so. And I am an Aries."

"Come on in," she motioned toward the curtain, "and let's have a look at what you've got."

They stepped into her parlor, which was even smaller than the first room, and dimly lit by candles. They sat down at a table covered with a top-to-floor black cloth. Tyrone spread his charts and tables over the cloth.

Mona studied them, nodding and muttering to herself. Tyrone clasped his hands in his lap and waited, controlling his nervousness.

"Very impressive," she said at last. "You computed this all by yourself?"

"Yes, ma'am, sort of." He smiled sheepishly. "But I got most of it from books and other stuff. I mean, I'm not an astrologer or anything."

"You're an Aries, which is something."

"Oh yeah, that. I just meant—"

"Go with it. Don't apologize."

He cleared his throat. "Okay. I had a little trouble with the, the emphemerisies."

"Ephemeries. They can be difficult, all those tables of the planets' positions and longitudes . . . I don't have a head for numbers myself. You've done pretty well with the cusps and decans, all in all, considering. I use a calculator—that makes it all easier." She reached under the table and brought up a pocket calculator and shoved it across to him. "No magic in those numbers, just numbers. No reason to ignore technological advances."

Tyrone examined the calculator as she examined him.

"You're a typical Aries, Tyrone. A lousy liar."

"Huh?" He looked up to see her smiling at him, her hands folded in front of her, her rings sparkling in the candlelight.

"So come clean. This isn't for a school project at all, is it?"

"Uh, well, oh gosh, it's—no, it's not. Sorry."

"Don't apologize. So?"

"So?"

"What's it for?"

Tyrone wrestled with himself, then realized he had no choice. "Well, Miss, uh . . ."

"Mona."

"Mona. I only said it was for school because, well, I thought that would be a better reason than the truth."

"Which is?"

"Okay." He pursed his lips and looked at her. "I want to chart a basketball team, and the truth is I didn't think you'd be interested in that."

"*Basketball!* Why not?"

" 'Cause it's just sports, and—"

"I've successfully predicted an entire season of dog racing." She leaned across the table toward him. "Not to mention last year's Super Bowl. Sports are like everything else—they're influenced by the stars. Given the correct astrological information, you can bet that Mona can figure it out."

"Gosh, I—"

"For a fee, of course."

"Oh. Sure, of course. I brought a little—"

"Not to you, not now. This one's a freebee. But for a team, I've got to charge."

"For sure!" Tyrone beamed. He liked her. "How'd you like to be our team astrologer?"

Mona rose slowly from the table and glided around the room, toying with the curls of her hair. "I don't know. I've never handled a team before. All those big goons running around in little shorts. Crowds, noise, sweatsocks . . ." She mumbled and pondered, then turned to focus her big eyes on Tyrone. "I have a big week ahead of me, actually. So I don't see how I could—"

"They're all Pisces."

"*All* Pisces?" She brightened. "You don't mean—"

"The Pythons!"

"You're on!"

6

The Pythons arrived at the Civic Arena locker room and began preparations for the night's game against New York.

Truth stepped up to his locker next to Driftwood and threw off his coat. "Hey, Driftwood, can you hear me with those earphones on?"

"I'm listening, you know, it's cool."

"But how you know what I'm saying?"

"I read lips."

Truth mouthed a silent obscenity.

"What?" Driftwood asked.

Setshot was the first to open his locker. "Hey! What happened to my uniform?" He stared into his empty locker.

"Maybe you been cut," Truth said.

Players laughed, but the laughter stopped when all the lockers were opened and turned out to be empty.

Jackhammer snapped his fingers. "Those unies musta been fated to be fumigated. It may be rude, but we'll be in the nude."

"Maybe the Hall of Fame wanted them," Rev. Jackson said.

Tyrone watched, grinning. "You guys looking for the uniforms?"

"Yeah," Truth said sternly. "What's going on?"

Through the door stepped Murray Sports, followed by Brockington, Cantrell, and team owner H. Sander Tilson. Crowding the hallway behind them were TV and newspaper reporters.

Tyrone strode in among the team and raised his

arms. "Listen, everybody! We got a special announcement from our owner."

Tilson put an arm around him, smiling his cherubic smile. The team gathered to listen. "Men, I'm really proud of you. It's been an uplifting experience watching this team play as it has for the most part lately—which is basic and simple and to my liking. And I'm sure all your fans are very grateful. And now—I have a little surprise!"

Moses leaned over to Running Hawk and whispered, "He gave us balloons when we won our first game."

Tilson's smile broadened and his facial pink deepened. "The Pittsburgh Pythons are changing their name. From now on we'll be called the Pittsburgh Pisces!"

"Pisces!" several of the players responded approvingly.

"And that's not all. Tyrone?"

Tyrone had ducked into the trainer's room, and now came back carrying a large box.

"Thank you, Tyrone," Tilson said, taking the box. "Moses? Would you come here, please?"

Moses glanced at the others, shrugged, and stepped forward. Tilson opened the box, dug into it, and pulled out a new jersey. He handed it to Moses, who held it up, drawing quick "ooohs!" and "aaahs!" from everyone.

The jersey, bearing his number 35, was shining, silvery white, with a black fish above the number, and aqua-colored letters, PISCES outlined in pink above the fish. Flashes came from the still cameras, and the TV cameras whirred.

"This is the new Pisces uniform," Tilson went on merrily, "designed to throw fear into anyone . . ." he darkened his expression ominously, then quickly brightened and threw his arm around Tyrone, ". . . except this one very special Aries!"

Tyrone grinned, then glanced up at the clock and discreetly left the locker room.

Tilson began passing out the rest of the uniforms. "So let's win this one for the fish!"

Tilson waved his fist and the team cheered and the players lunged for their new uniforms.

As Tilson tried to move out of the crowd, Murray Sports stuck a microphone into his face, Wally Cantrell looking over his shoulder. "Mr. Tilson, could you say a little more about this change, what it means?"

Ignoring that, Tilson abruptly turned back and, while reaching into his pocket, called, "I almost forgot! Balloons for everybody!" He tossed several handfuls of pink-and-aqua balloons into the air. Then he pushed his way out of the locker room and into the tunnel on the way to the court, trailed by Cantrell and several newsmen. "Wally, I want Tyrone to assume more responsibilities. I like that boy. Very basic and simple attitudes. Be a great engineer. See to it."

Cantrell nodded dubiously.

Murray Sports elbowed his way again to Tilson's side and stuck the microphone in front of him. "Sir, can you just tell us what this whole Pisces thing means?"

"It means they're all Pisces."

"But, but—oh well . . ." He turned to Cantrell. "Here, viewers, is the team's general manager. Mr. Cantrell, maybe you could shed some light on what's behind this sudden switch to—"

"No, I couldn't."

"Oh." Murray was left cranking his jaw wordlessly while his cameraman ground away at Cantrell's retreating back.

Edging past this crowd quickly, headed back toward the locker room and unnoticed, were Tyrone and Mona. Mona eyed the activity with some trepidation and pulled her black cape more tightly around her. Tyrone carried her attache case.

When they entered, the players had on their new uniforms and were admiring them, complimenting each other or looking at themselves in the mirrors.

"Hey, everybody!" Tyrone called. "Got somebody here I want you to meet! This is Miss Mona Mondieu." He paused. "Our new team astrologer!"

The team looked at her and at each other. Mona dipped into a deep curtsy.

"Foxy!" Truth said. "How you doing, Madam? Like the way you're dressed."

"Oh." She straightened and smoothed her dress.

"You must be Mr. Truth." She extended her hand. "How do you do, sir?"

"Fine, fine." He took her hand eagerly and squeezed. "Like the way you behave, too."

She quickly pulled her hand back. "My, such an excitable boy."

Brockington and Harry arrived in the room late, having had to fight their way through the crowd pouring into the arena, then the crowd pouring out of the tunnel.

"What is this?" Harry shouted, elbowing players aside. "You know the rules, no ladies in the locker room! Get rid of the dame!"

Brockington just stood open-mouthed.

"She's not a dame," Tyrone said, holding Harry back gently with two hands at his chest. "She's an astrologer here to teach us!"

"*Teach* us?" He turned to the coach. "Come on, Brockington, all this mystic stuff's gone far enough. Right? Right?"

Brockington looked around in a daze. Then he snapped out of it and took Harry's elbow to lead him aside. "Harry, one has to learn to relate to the revolutionary situation that we're facing as a team," he said confidentially. "*Relate* is the key word."

"Yeah, but Coach, *relate* should go only so far, and we got a dame in the locker room here, and . . ."

"Gentlemen!" Mona's voice commanded their attention. She tossed her cape back over her shoulders and strode up to Brockington and Harry. "Any objections if I brief the team for tonight's game?"

"Brief? Huh? What?" Harry stammered.

"Right on!" Brockington said, seizing the moment. "Sure! I can dig it! Groovy!" He raised a fist.

Harry folded his arms across his chest and faced the wall.

Mona stooped over her attache case, hiding it under her cape as she twirled the combination, opened it, and took out a thick folder. "Here, Tyrone, pass these around." She handed him copies of the team charts. As he passed them out, she went to the blackboard and began taping several astrological diagrams to it, humming to herself. "Now then." She turned to face the team. "You can all see these zodiac schematics, star charts on your opposition, and so forth, and you now have copies of your own charts in your hands."

Puzzled, they looked down at their charts and up at the blackboard and over at Mona.

She smiled and motioned toward the benches. "Could everyone please sit down?"

They did.

"Now!" Her voice became more assertive. "The problem's quite simple. You guys . . ." she tapped the blackboard charts, "are all blocked by a descendent *Leo*."

While she let that news sink in, Running Hawk mumbled, "Only descendent Leo I know is a guy from a long line of skid-row bums in the Bronx."

"Leo is a *sign*," Mona said, fixing Running Hawk with her big eyes, letting him know that she missed nothing, "not someone from New York. Tyrone, maybe you could amplify some of these things as I go along—in lingo these gentlemen could better comprehend."

"Right with you, Mona."

"Okay, item one. Now, what do you call it when all of you are out there running around, certain of the other guys constantly bumping into certain ones of you?"

"Pisces!" Setshot piped up.

Mona rolled her eyes.

"Matchups," Tyrone said.

"Right. Matchups." She licked the tip of a pencil and wrote the word on the back of her hand. "Fabulous. Okay now, Moses Guthrie, your matchup for tonight?"

"Haywood. Tough."

"Good. Haywood." She gazed off and murmured, "Haywood—the Taurus with the Capricorn influence. . . . As the night progresses, the Bull's energies will dissipate . . . the Goat will come on. . . . He's weak . . . Tyrone?"

"Moses, Mona means to give him plenty of slack in the first half, let him run himself out . . ."

"And take it to him late in the game," Moses put in. "Got it. Am I right, Mona?"

"Absolutely." She smiled coyly. "You're right on top of it, Moses. He'll run out of steam, or as you might put it, gas."

"I'm hip."

She cast her eyes over the team and caught sight of Benny and Kenny. "Oooh, the twins! What fascinating raw material!"

They looked down at their chart.

"May I ask you, ma'am," Benny said, "what's all this about stars working in con, con—"

"*Conjunction,* Benny."

He looked up, startled. "How you know I'm Benny?"

"Mona knows." She gave him her mysterious smile. "Because you're two minutes older. It was a snap, spotting the difference in your rising signs."

"But, but . . ."

"That's a first," Kenny said, waving his chart. "Give you credit for that."

"Thank you." She lowered her head demurely.

"But what's all this jive got to do with basketball —I mean, I understand how Moses might move on Haywood the second half, but that's not so new, 'cause Moses always got more gas than anybody."

Titters ran through the group.

Tyrone stuck up a hand. "What she's saying is, that when you two guys are out on the court, you—"

"You become *one,*" Mona put in quickly. "One great player instead of two ordinary ones." She peered at them. "Think about it."

They wrinkled their brows in concentration.

Rev. Jackson had his brow wrinkled too, but with more suspicions than thought. His look was almost a scowl as she approached him, but she spoke before he could.

"Reverend Jackson, your chart indicates you're in a period of trying to overcome a weakness."

"Oh yeah?"

"Yes."

"Well, generally I got the Lord coverin' up for me —er-uh, watching over me. So tell me," he folded his arms across his chest, "just what *is* my weakness, child?"

"I'm quoting—'It is shown in weakness, it is raised in power'—from First Corinthians."

His mouth dropped open. "Fifteenth chapter, forty-third verse! My, my, my!" Now he was intrigued. "And your parallel is?"

"Turnovers, Reverend, and I don't mean the apple kind."

"Aha! So the stars say I'm not handling the ball good?"

"Dribbling, to be precise. Dribbling too much. You know the quotation, 'Out of weakness . . .' "

" 'We are made strong!' " He clapped and then raised his hands high. "Mondieu! Lordy, lordy. Praise *Him!* Imagine *that!* I do believe I *believe!"*

Mona smiled proudly and moved on. She headed over to Bullet, who, seeming oblivious, was salting a hard-boiled egg. "You don't talk, Bullet, but you have a lot to say, hmm?" She met his eyes as they came up. "Your chart shows no blockage on the court tonight."

He raised his eyebrows.

"None."

He gave her his most charming smile, moved his hands deftly, and made the egg disappear.

"Great," she said as she turned away, "use that magic against the Knicks tonight." She moved along the bench. "Jackhammer and Running Hawk." She nodded at them and then gazed off. "Interesting. Both of your charts show—well, to put it simply, Jupiter and Mercury both indicate you should be on the defensive tonight."

They looked at each other.

"Say no more," Jackhammer said, "just show us the floor."

"And you, Driftwood," she sidled along, "a triple water sign. Go with the flow."

"Right on," he said softly without removing the headphones. "But it's hard swimming upstream."

She waggled her finger to indicate removal of the phones. He pulled them off. "Go with the flow, I said. *Upstream* is not it."

"Oh, right. Got you." He replaced the phones. "Slipping out of practice with lip-synch, I guess."

"And you, Setshot," she continued. "Mars is the God of War, and a very unusual configuration relates to your water sign right now—in your twelfth house."

"Come again, ma'am? I only lived in three houses, not counting my sister's."

She chuckled. "Okay, I'll catch you later with more about that." She looked around. "All right, team—all of you—for the past few months your Jupiter has been in a fixed position, and therefore you have been very lucky. I mean *lucky*. But now Mercury is in retrograde and things won't be all that easy." She watched some faces fall. "But there are positive aspects also, so don't worry about it. Worrying is destructive anyway, especially under *your* sign. And remember: when you're with Mona, the stars are with you. Now . . ." She flashed a wide smile and waved a fist, "Go get 'em, Pisces!"

They roared out, stomping and cheering and clapping.

As they streamed into the tunnel, Brockington was trying to work his way back. He let them pass and came up to Mona. He looked down at his chart and shook his head. "Just between us, Miss Mondieu, does this stuff really work?"

"For you, Mr. Brockington, it works like this—I've studied the referees' charts and they're both in evil moods, or will be. Don't challenge them tonight."

"Who, me?" He was shocked at the suggestion.

"Keep it in mind."

Harry rushed up and took Brockington by the elbow. "Come on, Coach, game time! We only got two minutes!"

As they moved off down the tunnel, following the team toward the court, Harry glanced back, then asked Brockington softly, "Did you find out where the stargazer parked her broom?"

"Can it, Harry. This is serious!"

Tyrone led Mona to a special chair at the end of the bench, and Brockington gathered the team around, pepping them up with his customary "tough get going" talk, and sent out a starting five of Moses, Jackson, Bullet, Running Hawk, and Driftwood.

The two starting teams lined up around the jump circle. But then the Knicks began really noticing the new uniforms.

"Hey, man," said Knicks center McAdoo to Jackson, "where'd you guys get *those?* They're all *right!"*

Jackson touched his uniform proudly. Similar observations came from around the circle, and Jackson's Pisces mates fingered their jerseys with satisfaction.

The referee blew his whistle. "All right, show's over," he said irritably, "let's get this game started!"

Just as he tossed the ball up, Jackson asked McAdoo, "What's your sign?" Having distracted him, Jackson leaped to win the tip.

Moses took it and dribbled to the forecourt, Haywood on him tight. He started a drive to his right, then backed off. In another situation, without the pregame admonitions from Mona, he would have continued in for the shot. Now he passed off to Bullet, who was open at the top of the key. He hesitated.

"Shoot!" Mona yelled from the bench. "No blockage!"

But he bounced it in to Jackson, cutting across the lane. He dribbled once and the ball was poked away. The Knicks launched a fast break, Butch Beard taking it in for the lay-up.

"That's your weakness!" Mona hollered as Jackson came back upcourt. "The stars don't lie!" She added, under her breath. "I may, but they don't."

The Pisces brought the ball up. Moses tried to drive, got past Haywood, but was confronted by an alert McAdoo. He looped a pass back out to Running Hawk. His hook was blocked by Haywood, and New York took it over.

Back at their end, McAdoo drove around Jackson and pulled up for a fade-away ten-footer. Driftwood sailed across to block it.

The Pisces controlled again. Moses slowed the tempo down, trying to give everybody a chance to concentrate on what they had been told. He handed off to Running Hawk and set a screen for him.

But Hawk called "number three" and passed in to

Jackson again, who seemed open and dribbled for the hoop. McAdoo plucked it right off his fingers, and the Knicks took off for another fast-break basket.

Mona glanced at Tyrone, who was biting his lip. "You know the term, 'retrograde,' in astrology?"

"Something about the backward motion of planets."

"Right. And what we're watching here is retrograde basketball."

Brockington scrambled down to her in front of the bench. "Should I call a time-out?"

"No." She jumped up and called out, "Shoot now! Shoot the thing, Bullet!"

Bullet and Running Hawk exchanged passes outside the key, neither willing to take the shot, even though the New York defense was collapsing off them to crowd up the middle.

Driftwood shook loose and got open beside the lane. Hawk fed him, and he tried a short hook that bounced off the rim.

Moses battled Haywood underneath for the rebound. Moses controlled, faked Haywood into the air, then went up for the dunk that put the Pisces on the scoreboard at last.

"Yes, yes, *yes!*" Brockington yelled.

The Pisces fell back smartly on defense. Bullet crowded the New York guard, Monroe, with the ball. He had solid position between Monroe and the basket. Monroe ran into him for an obvious charge.

The referee whistled, but called a blocking foul on Bullet.

The Pisces groaned.

Brockington jumped off the bench. "Are you *nuts?*" he hollered at the ref.

Tyrone, remembering Mona's warning, called down, "Wait, Coach!"

But Mona restrained him. "He has to operate by his own chart." She shook her head. "My words are like pearls cast before swine—the story of my life."

Brockington stormed out. "You didn't see that! You weren't anywhere near the play, ref!"

The ref spun around. "Another word from you— it's a 'T.' "

"What?"

The ref blew his whistle and made a "T" with his hands, signaling a technical foul on the coach.

Brockington stuffed a towel into his mouth as the ref led McAdoo to the foul line to shoot the technical.

Mona stood and beckoned to Tyrone. "Think your team can spare you for a little bit? The situation calls for a visual-aid demonstration. Let's set it up."

Tyrone followed Mona down the sideline toward the tunnel, wincing as he saw yet another potential shot bobbled by the Reverend. When they left the floor, New York led, 15–4, with half the first quarter gone.

After a while, New York went into a shooting slump. They really cooled off and couldn't hit anything and the Pisces began chipping away. Bad as it still was, it would have been much worse otherwise. The teams left the court at halftime with the score, Knicks 62, Pisces 47.

The sweat-drenched, disheartened Pisces players dragged into the locker room, taking the towels handed out by Tyrone as they entered. They collapsed in groans and moans onto the benches, muttering angrily and shaking their heads.

Suddenly all their heads were brought up to attention by a rapping at the far end of the room.

"Gentlemen." There, tapping with a pointer on the side of the overhead TV monitor, stood Mona. "Please observe."

What they saw on the screen was a frozen image of the scoreboard showing them down by fifteen.

"And please observe further, here. I have a few things to—"

"Hey!" Brockington stalked into the room, stopped, looked around, and frowned. "What're you doing?" He advanced on Mona. "Now *look*, lady, you can pull all the magic you want and read all the charts you want, but I'm still the head coach of this team!"

"Right!" She held him back with the tip of her pointer, like a fencer with an épée. "Stop racing your motor." She steered him around and caused him to sit down on a bench with the others. "Now then." She wiggled her pointer up at the monitor. "For openers, there's three free ones up on the board, compliments of *you,* Mr. Head Coach Brockington."

"One! One only. One 'T' is all I—"

"One technical foul, and another lay-up because you distracted the refs with your nonsense so they missed another obvious charging foul on New York, which would have eliminated the basket."

"Whew!" Truth said admiringly. "The lady's on the case!"

Brockington wrung his hands. "But you can't let the refs get away with bad calls—can you?"

"Foretold is forewarned. Roll it, Tyrone. Watch the screen, please, gentlemen."

They watched while the video replay came on. The action showed Benny and Kenny operating independent of each other on opposite sides of the court—ineffective on both offense and defense.

"Hold it." The action on the screen stopped. "What's the matter with you two?" She glared at the twins. "In one ear and out the other three?" They hung their heads. *"Conjunction,* remember? Together, *one* great player—separate, two amateurs. Buck up, fellows, I'm not putting you down, just *advising* you."

They nodded.

"Okay, roll some more." The screen showed Moses and Haywood going one-on-one, Haywood dominating for a while, then, as the action skipped forward, Moses coming on, slipping by him for a few shots, holding him off on the defensive end. "See how you're starting to dominate late in the half, Moses? Haywood's fading."

"I see it."

She smiled at him. "Now challenge him hard and the second half's all yours. Feeling good, aren't you?"

He grinned up at her. "Second half's usually mine anyway."

"Even more so this time, right?"

"Right. I got you."

"Now then." On the screen was a rapid montage of Jackson's fumbling routines. Every time he tried to dribble, the ball was knocked away. "Need I say—"

"I'm with you, Mondieu," the Reverend said. "Keep it off the floor."

"For tonight, right."

"Hey!" Jackhammer leaned forward. "Everybody rhymin' ruins my timin'!"

Mona chuckled at him. "Okay—your way."

Even Jackhammer was forced to laugh.

But Brockington was not. He had been chewing the ends of his fingers as he sensed the leadership of his team slipping away. Now he could contain himself no longer. He jumped up in agitation. "Now just hold the phone!"

Mona pantomimed holding a receiver to her ear.

He shook a finger. "If you have all the answers, then tell me how we're supposed to make up fifteen points in the second half. Huh?"

She smiled patiently, then nodded. She pointed to the monitor. The view was of the concentrating face of Setshot at the free-throw line.

Setshot blinked several times as he looked at it. Suddenly he held his eyes wide open. "Fouls."

"Yup."

"Free throws."

"Yup."

He narrowed his eyes and clenched his hands on his thighs. "I'm ready!"

"Mmm-hmm."

The second half opened with New York controlling the ball. McAdoo took a pass down low. Haywood set a pick to take out Moses. McAdoo cut around it for the basket.

But he never saw Setshot. The little man had positioned himself perfectly, and McAdoo ran over him, knocking him backward and sending him skidding across the floor on his rear end.

As the referee whistled the charging foul, Setshot, dazed, slowly picked himself up and walked down the court. "Fouls . . ." he muttered, "free throws . . . I'm ready . . ."

Bullet dribbled up, holding three fingers high to indicate a play. He faked a pass to Setshot, then bounced it in to the Reverend. Pisces cut to either side of him. Jackson controlled his urge to dribble, faked to the first two men, then handed off to Moses who rammed it into the net.

A few moments later, they ran the same play, Jackson passing off this time to Bullet, who laid it up, spinning it off his finger.

Tyrone leaned over to Mona. "I think they're starting to get the point."

"Yup. And we're going to get the *points*."

The crowd began to come alive as the Pisces began to move. At New York's end of the floor, the Knicks ran a weave, and guard Beard ran into Setshot, sending him caroming into a bunch of photographers at the end line.

Setshot was on his feet quickly. "Fouls, free throws, ready . . ."

New York was over the team-foul limit, and Setshot went to the line. A look of deep satisfaction crossed his face as he swished the shot and heard the applause of the crowd.

Shortly, at the Pisces end, Setshot was again sent flying—he didn't even know who ran into him. He tumbled into the first row of seats and was helped to his feet by cheering people whose faces were blurs to him.

At the New York end of the court, Setshot was blasted head-over-heels by three Knicks who seemed to converge on him.

The crowd was growing wilder with its applause and cheers for the downed little man. This time Harry hurried off the bench and over to him. Setshot was having trouble getting up. He had lumps over both eyes like a battered boxer.

"Hang tough, Setshot," Harry said, checking around the bruises with his fingers. "Some people got height, but you got heart!"

"Erg."

He made yet another free throw, even though he could barely see the rim.

From then on, what might have been a nightmare to Setshot was a pure delight to the crowd. The game went on with heightening intensity as the Pisces concentrated, played well together, and steadily narrowed the gap. And every once in a while—often, actually—Setshot was sent flying, tumbling, sliding, spinning from collisions with Knicks.

He went down with a thigh injury. Harry attended him like a battlefield medic, spraying the muscle with pain-soothing ethyl chloride and wrapping it with an Ace bandage.

He dislocated a finger. Harry snapped it back in place, sprayed it, and wrapped it with tape.

An elbow to the head knocked him out. Harry wakened him with smelling salts and an ice pack. "Okay, trooper," Harry said, "back in action."

His ear was cut, his trunks were torn, he lost a shoe for a while. Harry kept rushing out to tape him together. After a while he was sprayed and wrapped nearly from head to toe.

And all the time he kept making free throws and the Pisces kept cutting down the margin. Reverend Jackson was passing off well, Truth was driving, Running Hawk was scoring hooks, and Moses was hitting from everywhere. And they were hustling and pressing on defense.

New York reached 100, 105, 110—with the Pisces right behind them: 95, 102, 108.

Finally there were but twenty seconds left. New York led, 115–114. The Knicks had the ball out of bounds at their end. All they had to do was pass the ball in and run out the clock.

Beard had the ball out of bounds. He looked for somebody to pass to. The Pisces swarmed on defense. Finally McAdoo broke free near the center line and took the pass in. Beard cut past him and McAdoo handed him the ball. Beard dribbled in and out among the chasing Pisces as the seconds ticked off.

Somewhere in the middle of the frantic pursuit, Setshot sensed the inevitable. He tucked his elbows in to protect his midsection and put his hands over his face. "Fouls . . . free throws . . ."

Beard was cornered. He managed to pass off to McAdoo, who turned and slammed immediately into Setshot. Setshot slid headlong across the floor, ending up in a heap under the scorer's table.

The referee called the foul on McAdoo. The crowd went into a frenzy. The Pisces went under the scorer's table to fetch poor Setshot. They dragged him out and stood him up. Harry rubbed him all over with a towel as if drying him at a carwash.

"Fouls . . ." Setshot's voice was barely audible through his puffy lips, and his eyes were closed. " . . . free throws . . ."

They talked to him, pleaded with him, held him up, tried to pry open his eyes.

"You go to the line . . ." Benny said.

"To try for two . . ." Kenny said.

"Two free shots . . . said Running Hawk.

"And we're behind by *one point* . . ."

"One second left . . ." Truth said.

"You got two tries, so open your eyes . . ." Jackhammer said.

"You can win it for us!" Moses said.

Slowly Setshot opened his eyes and tried to focus. Slowly he pushed his teammates away. Slowly he started to walk toward the Pisces' free-throw line. He staggered and wavered, but his narrowly opened eyes never left the basket.

The crowd was on its feet, but hushed.

Black and blue and wrapped in bandages, Setshot toed the line. The referee handed him the ball. He stumbled to the left, but straightened out and recovered. His knees buckled, but gradually they firmed and held.

Shaking, dizzy, half blind, Setshot cocked the ball in his hands and sent it up. It hit the back of the rim and bounced high, then dropped through. The crowd cheered, then quickly quieted again.

Setshot staggered backward. Driftwood and Truth caught him and steered him back to the line.

He sent up his two-hander. The ball rolled around and around the rim. And dropped through.

The crowd erupted. The din was deafening and undiminishing. New York inbounded the ball and the final buzzer sounded—with the Pisces the victors, 116–115.

Setshot, asleep or unconscious, was hoisted aloft, prone, and carried toward the tunnel by his cheering teammates, Mona Mondieu among them.

7

The ritual of jogging at dawn has its difficulties and discouragements, and for Halsey Tilson, the ritual was done in the deserted private park adjoining his childhood home, the estate on which the family mansion was located and where his brother, H. Sander, now lived. It was the dark bitterness over his brother's unfair occupation of that nearby mansion that drove Halsey to run—not the pudgy shape of his body.

So this morning Halsey was wobbling along in his warm-up suit, covered with sweat and mind-warped with strain and rancor. He was puffing up a minor hill in the acreage of manicured lawn.

From behind him came an electronic whir, which interrupted his solitude, and shortly beside him appeared his lawyer, Friesman, seated in a golf cart. He was fresh and neatly combed and dressed in a black suit.

"Mr. Tilson! Mr. Tilson! I've got it!"

Halsey didn't look over, but continued his weary pace. "Got what? Ringworm?"

"No, sir, no. A loophole to shut down your brother's team! It's right here in the arena-leasing agreement." He pulled out a document from his pocket and began to read, steering erratically: " 'The party hereby known as the—' "

"*Shorthand,* Friesman!" Halsey gasped. "You happen to be trespassing on Tilson family property and you're interrupting . . ." He was forced to take several deep breaths. ". . . my communion with my past." He

103

crested the hill and continued gratefully on the downward slope. "Now spit it out!"

Friesman nodded like a woodpecker. "Briefly, the arena's leased to the Pittsburgh *Pythons*," he said rapidly. "Inasmuch as they're now known as the Pisces, I believe we can void the lease and they'll have no place to play!" He smiled as gaily as a man of his gray disposition could manage. "Good tactics, wouldn't you say?"

"I would *not* say! Now halt that cart!" Halsey stopped, his whole body heaving, and Friesman stopped the cart beside him. "Out!" Without waiting for compliance, Halsey reached in and yanked the lawyer out of the cart, spinning him aside. "Ten-*hut!*"

Friesman snapped to attention, trembling, not daring even to straighten his tie.

Halsey clasped his hands behind him and paced back and forth. Then he stopped and faced Friesman jaw to jaw. "Get this straight, soldier: leases are penny-ante at this stage of the game! Do you know what this stage of the game is?"

"Why, uh, I should think, I guess . . ."

"We are *down to the wire!*"

"Sir?"

Halsey swaggered back and forth. "It's like this, mister—in the Marines we had a saying: go for the throat! Assault!" He spun around to the quavering Friesman and thrust his hands suddenly at him as if delivering a bayonet. Friesman stumbled backward.

"Ten-*hut!*" Friesman stiffened again. "Now here this! We have to move on the *generals,* you jellyfish!"

"Sir? Who . . . who . . ."

"Who, who, who, *who.* Who *is* the general leading the Pisces?"

"Br . . . Br . . ."

"Spit it out!"

"Brocking . . . ton?"

"Ooof!" Halsey turned away in disgust.

"Do we assault Coach Brockington?"

"No, you idiot, that would only help them to get that buffoon outta there! *Think,* shyster! Who's *really* leading them?"

"The . . . the astrology woman?"

"Aha!" Halsey stuck his jaw in Friesman's face and grinned wickedly.

"Do something with her?"

"Yes, yes, come on!" Halsey beckoned with his fingers.

Friesman concentrated hard. "Let's see . . . remove . . ."

"Keep talking, come on."

"Remove her . . ."

"Out with it!"

"Kidnap her!" Friesman's eyes widened at the thought.

"Right! Brilliant idea, Friesman. Your idea, of course, not mine."

"Uh . . ."

"Go for the throat, of course!" Halsey gripped Friesman's tie and twisted it. "Mona Mondieu. Absolutely brilliant mind you have."

Color returned to Friesman's face as Halsey released the tie. He straightened his tie and gradually regained a semblance of composure and dignity. "Mr. Tilson, I believe I know just the two men for the job—experts."

"Very good, Friesman," Halsey purred. "And of course you will take care that my name is not involved with his little caper of *yours*." He chuckled meanly. "Botch this one, fella, and I'll see to it that you're bundled off to the Legal Aid Society where you can work with the alligators that'll chew your guts out in night court!"

"Oh yes, understood, sir! Absolutely. I'll handle it!"

"Good lad." He patted the attorney on the head and slid into the golf cart. With a patrician wave of his arm, he said, "Now, give me ten good laps behind the cart—with spirit!"

Chortling, Halsey hummed off in the cart. Friesman trotted behind him, loosening his tie.

Another night, another game, another victory for the Pisces—a 107–97 win over the San Antonio Spurs. It was a tough game, requiring special concentration on defense. Moses scored only 20 points—low for him—but blocked seven shots and took down eighteen rebounds. The twins worked well together, and Bullet hit a crucial series of jumpers in the fourth quarter.

A group of fans, mostly girls, waited outside the players' entrance to congratulate their idols. Among the group were Ola and Brandy. Both were excited, but Ola was absolutely giddy with what she had seen and what she anticipated.

"Girl, did they stick it to the Spurs tonight!" Ola crowed. She slapped palms with Brandy. "And my man Bullet—eighteen points! You see that? I declare, I can't wait to talk to my man tonight. Gonna pat that slick head of his. I know he's gonna be happy."

"You ever gonna ask him about Jamaal?"

"These things take time, Brandy. I mean, we got a lot of other things to talk about besides fixing you up with Jamaal Truth. Anyway, Bullet will be rappin' so strong I can never get a word in edgewise."

"Yeah, well, that's something I sure don't understand, girl. How he talks to you so quick and so long, and nobody else ever heard him open his mouth."

Ola smiled secretively.

A shriek came from the girls nearest the door. Moses and Tyrone came out and Moses was immediately mobbed for autographs. He obliged graciously as they pushed slowly through the crowd.

"We're on the roll now," Tyrone said as he tried to wedge a path for them both. "And they wanna do a feature on the team for 'Wide World of Sports' next week."

Near the far edge of the crowd, Moses felt somebody watching him—a different kind of vibration from the rest. He looked up from his mechanical business of autographing. There stood Toby, not smiling, a determined look on her pretty face.

Moses had met her before, a couple of times, and had a chance to talk to her briefly. He had found her charming. She was attractive to look at, of course. But she was also serious without being somber, which appealed to him because he also was a serious person. So he was pleased to see her standing there, and, while Tyrone lingered behind to bask in the fallout of adoration for Moses, he went up to her.

Before he could say anything, Toby cut in. "Mr. Guthrie, we have to talk. It's very important."

"Sure, fine." He motioned behind him. "I was just gonna give Tyrone a ride home. So you come along, we can talk on the—"

"Alone."

Now he noticed for the first time how completely serious she was.

Tyrone came trotting up to join them, then stopped short, sensing something. "Uh, listen, you guys. I'll get a ride with Setshot." He started to leave, then turned back. "Moses?"

"Yeah, buddy?"

"Think about your chart, okay? You know . . . the part about confrontation off the court." He waved. "See you later."

Moses watched him leave, then turned to Toby. "Okay. Alone. I'll be happy to give you a ride home, Miss Millman. My car is right over here."

He guided her to his Rolls, held the door open politely for her, then got in himself.

They both were silent as he drove out of the parking lot, headed downtown. After a time, he looked at her and smiled pleasantly. "Whatever's on your mind, you're welcome to say it."

A bit flustered by his polite treatment, she hesitated.

"Whenever you're ready."

She took a deep breath. "Okay. Look," she turned in her seat to face him, "you've got Tyrone believing that all he has to do is grow into a seven-foot freak and have his chart done and all his troubles will be over for the rest of his life."

"Is that so?"

"Yes, that's so!" Her anger built. She had stored it up for a long time, watching Tyrone change and worrying about him. "He just has to hang around you guys and be in the locker room to learn all that

locker-room talk and live and die for the Pisces and
dream of living that way, being like you, having nothing but basketball to—"

"Hey, now wait a minute, li'l sister—"

"I'm not your little sister! And keep your eyes on
the road. I'm gonna tell you frankly, I don't give a
hang about the Pythons or the Pisces or any of that.
What I care about is Tyrone! I've been caring about
Tyrone for a long time, and I'm not gonna let him
go wrong now!"

"I'd like to tell you something about Tyrone. Tyrone is—"

"I'll tell *you* about Tyrone! Tyrone is a good kid,
and bright. But Tyrone is not paying attention to his
schoolwork lately. And that's where it's really at in
this world, Mr. Guthrie—education to get somewhere,
not just a dead end as some kind of athlete. He
doesn't do his chores. And that means something, too.
Responsibility. He's got his head in the clouds. And
it's because of you."

Moses glanced over at her just long enough to see
that there were tears in her eyes. He was stung by her
words, but felt it better not to answer them just now.

"He is not gonna get paid a million dollars to run
around in his underwear," she went on, her voice
cracking. "The only way he'll go to college is to get
a scholarship based on good grades. That is his way
out, the only way. And he won't get that by trying
to follow in the footsteps of an overgrown freak who
can only count in twos."

"Meaning me."

"Well . . ." she turned away, "yeah, I guess."

He turned down a side street and started past a
junior high school "Hey, wait a minute." He braked
to a quick stop, backed up a few feet, and parked.
"Come with me, okay?"

He got out and went to the rear and opened the
trunk.

She didn't move.

He took a basketball out of the trunk, closed it,
and walked up to her door. She was sitting stiffly,

staring straight ahead. He opened the door carefully. "Please come with me."

Reluctantly she got out, and, hands jammed into her coat pockets and shoulders hunched, followed him.

They walked around behind the school to the playground. Streetlights lit the area dimly. He led her through the playground gate and onto the empty basketball court.

Then he stopped and stared at the hoop, which had a woven chain net. He bounced the ball a few times without looking at it. She watched him. There was a curious new kind of intensity to his face that she hadn't seen before.

"I played on a court just like this when I was a kid," he said softly. "Other kids would be out partying. I was out here practicing and practicing by myself until I was too wiped out to see straight. And it wasn't because I was dumb. It was because I cared about myself." He bounced the ball, never taking his eyes off the hoop. "I was tall, but I was clumsy. And I hated being laughed at. Nobody likes being laughed at. And everybody has to deal with it in their own way. My way was here. On a basketball court. I didn't know if I'd make it work or not. But I knew that how you played here was one way you got respect. In my neighborhood, this was a battleground. Not with knives or fists. With a basketball."

He hoisted the ball over his head and sent up a shot. The ball clanked through the net. He trotted in to retrieve it.

Toby sat down on a rickety bench by the fence. He walked over to her and looked down into her eyes. "I had to learn to squeeze out whatever talent I had for my own future. It was not play. It was serious business. I had to learn to walk and lean on air—always jumping, learning how to float and move. Whether I grew up to be a freak that ran around in his underwear or not, it was my way."

He turned and tossed the ball up against the backboard, then ran in under it, leaped to intercept the rebound at its highest point, and slammed the ball into the chains backward over his head—each movement showing the grace and skill that had made him famous.

Then he walked back to her. "I learned to listen to the rhythm of my body. I learned to push myself, and how far, how long I could do it. I had to see how far I could go. I had to know. I had my dreams —just like Tyrone has his. People laugh at dreams. The only reason nobody laughs at me now is because I made 'em real."

He left her sitting there and went onto the court. For the next fifteen minutes he put on a solo performance—no crowd, no reporters, only Toby to see. But it was as if even she wasn't there. It was a performance for himself. He dribbled, spun, drove, slammed the ball into the chains forward and backward; he faked and moved and sprang, sending soft jumpshots in from the corners, from the free-throw circle, from deep, from short. He palmed the ball and soared with it, laying it in deftly off the backboard or jamming it down into the hoop. He dribbled the ball behind his back, through his legs, tossed it high onto the backboard and leaped to tip it in.

He displayed his own variations of every move made on a basketball court, by small men or big men, by shooters or ball-handlers. He showed her everything Moses Guthrie could do, in an intense drama of concentration and skill and stamina. Her eyes were riveted on him.

Finally he came over to her, sweat dripping off his face and staining his shirt. His trousers were wet, his shoes scuffed. He met her eyes. "That's what I do," he said quietly. "And I do it because that's the best thing I can do in this whole world. And a long time ago, it was just my dream."

Tyrone heard her come in and quickly left his homework to meet her. It was late for him to be up, but he wanted to see her. He ran out into the hall.

"Hey, sis, how'd it go?"

"How'd what go?" she said casually, hanging her coat on a hook.

"With Moses, I mean. You guys talk?"

"Yes, we talked."

"Well . . ." He didn't know if he should pursue the subject.

She brushed past him, then turned back, her hands on her hips. "Tyrone, tell me something. What do you think of Moses Guthrie?"

"Moses? Wow, he's the greatest player I ever—"

"I don't mean as a basketball player. I mean really"

"Gee." He studied his hands, then looked up at her. "Well, if you want the truth, I'd say he's just about the nicest person I ever met. I mean, I don't know how to explain it. It's not just that he's nice to me. And maybe nice isn't even the right word. But even to all the other guys, you know. He *cares* about them, about the team, about the guys themselves. Even about old Brockington. He *thinks* a lot, you know what I mean?"

"Mmm."

"I mean, if I could grow up to be like anybody in the whole world, it'd be like—" He stopped himself. He was aware of her discomfort about his interest in basketball. "Why you asking?"

"We're going to have dinner tomorrow night."

"Gee! Gosh! Wow! I mean, um—" he glanced at the floor "—that's sure nice, sis. You looking forward to it?"

She smiled and patted his head and went off to her room.

The City of Pittsburgh was transformed. The Pisces kept on winning, and they kept on creeping up through the standings. What would have been an idle dream a couple of months before had become a reality: the Pisces made the play-offs. And the magic spread through the populace. Everybody talked about the Pisces, and special banners and placards were displayed everywhere. The sports pages were filled with news of the team and player profiles; TV led off newscasts with announcements of the latest Pisces successes.

A group of marathon runners headed through the

suburbs bound for the city. They passed a sign reading: "Welcome to Pittsburgh—Population 458,651." Under the words somebody had spray-painted: "Home of the Pisces." The runners were wearing beanies topped with spinning propellers. The propellers were not blades, however, but fish.

The Pisces not only reached the play-offs, but advanced. They won a tough two-out-of-three with Washington in the first round.

In a small restaurant near the city's fringe, a family was eating lunch. They were eating trout, bass, and perch. A sign on the door read, "No Meat Until Play-offs." But a line had been drawn through "Play-offs" and "Finals" had been added.

A little boy in the family whispered to his father, who nodded. The boy was reluctant. The father nudged him. The boy got up and took his plate shyly to the rear, to a small table for two. There sat Moses and Toby, enjoying a quiet lunch where they thought they wouldn't be disturbed.

The boy held out the plate. Moses didn't notice him at first. Toby touched Moses' arm and cocked her head toward the boy. Moses smiled at him, took the plate, pulled out a felt-tipped pen, and autographed the shiny perch.

They had been seeing a lot of each other—as much as they could under the circumstances. Moses and Toby got together whenever Moses was not playing out of town or practicing, which was most of the time. As rough as the regular season was, play-off time was worse. The pressure grew. But when they could, they met, and talked, and laughed, and shared what they were doing.

And they quickly grew close. Just how close was not something either of them tried to measure for a while. But at least many of their thoughts were about each other, when they were together and when they were not.

But Moses was not—could not afford to be—distracted from the game. Beyond the stars and charts and advisories from Mona, Moses was the key to the team. It was his talent and drive and condition that got them through the tough spots, and the play-offs were filled with tough spots. Washington had taken them to overtime in two of the three games, and Moses put in the winning shots both times.

And then Phoenix. The Suns were rough and defensive-minded. The Pisces battled them even in low-scoring games for the first four of the best-of-five semifinals.

A large contingent of fans followed the Pisces to their away games, but those who couldn't travel were just as interested. A giant fish-shaped billboard was erected in the center of the city. At the top of the billboard was, "PISCES PLAY-OFF PROGRESS." And beneath that was recorded: "PISCES 2—PHOENIX 2."

The final game was in Phoenix. It was carried on TV and radio, so the large crowd gathered at the billboard that night knew the outcome. Still they were there to see the result displayed larger than life.

And when the number for Pisces changed from "2" to "3", the hundreds of townspeople—including several old men in wheelchairs—cheered as mightily as if they hadn't just seen the dramatic game on the screen, and hadn't known that Setshot had won the game with five straight free throws in the final minute.

The excitement was no less at the retirement home itself, from which many of the wheelchair residents were taken to attend home games. A male attendant in a white uniform came running down the hall toward some screeching that came from an intersecting corridor. He met another attendant emerging from a room.

"Come on!" called the first. "Sweets has another nurse cornered."

The second man fell in beside him at a trot. "Maybe she told him he couldn't go to the finals."

"Doubt it. Sweets has become a Romeo lately."

"This whole place has been bananas since the Pisces made the play-offs."

They turned the corner and bumped into three old ladies lined up in a high-kick exercise.

"Hey!" the attendant shouted, bouncing off the first lady. "What's going on?"

"Cheerleading practice," said the lady. "We gotta

lead the men in special yells here before they go to watch the Lakers."

"Sweets with you?"

"Oh no." The lady adjusted her knee socks. "He's having a romantic interlude with Nurse Mindy Nix."

The attendants took off again, headed for the screeching for help they now knew came from Nurse Nix.

"Our only hope to save this place," panted the first attendant, "is that Los Angeles takes it in a quick four."

The Los Angeles Lakers had swept their series against Portland and Denver, losing only one game. Kareem Abdul-Jabbar had been magnificent all year, and even better in the play-offs. He had been upstoppable on offense, averaging thirty points a game, and on defense completely intimidating anyone trying to work in close.

Beating the Lakers would require the ultimate in team play by the Pisces, a dedicated effort to use everybody on the court and Mona would have to work overtime on her charts. And the charts became more and more valuable. No longer could she entrust them to her combination-lock attache case. She took to keeping them in a sterling silver strongbox.

In the first two games, Kareem destroyed the Pisces almost single-handed, scoring 47 in the first and 55 in the second, and blocking seventeen shots. The Pisces never got to within ten points of the Lakers at any time during either game.

Then Jabbar cooled off, the stars and planets appeared to work better for the Pisces, and, led by Bullet from the outside and Jackson from the inside—capitalizing on his quickness against Jabbar—along with Moses' steadiness from everywhere, the Pisces took the next two in squeakers. Setshot won one with a free throw at the buzzer. Running Hawk hit two long hooks, and Kenny and Benny ran two sensational fast breaks to win the second in the last two minutes.

And before each game, Mona arrived in her special silver limousine. As one man stood guard, the other opened the rear door of the limo, hauled out the silver strongbox, and escorted Mona and the charts into the building.

Between the games, when Moses could make it, he and Toby spent time together. They took long rides in the country, away from the hubbub of the city and the basketball court. They held hands and wandered through amusement parks and zoos and museums, and lunched in small out-of-the-way places. They sat admiring waterfalls in the woods of the Allegheny Mountains. They rode the cable car up the Duquesne Incline to get a spectacular view of Pittsburgh from Mt. Washington.

They talked about Tyrone and each other and the importance of striving for a sense of peace within oneself. They did not talk about basketball. Toby was curious and wanted to know everything about the game, and about Moses' special thoughts and attitudes on the basketball court. But he ruled the topic off-limits—until after the final series with the Lakers.

"I concentrate so much on that," he told her, "it's like I'm near an overload. I gotta have a break from it, with you. Afterwards, I'll tell you everything."

And she would hug him and say she understood and feel warm with the promise of spending time with him after the season.

For indeed the time had been promised. Their feelings for each other had deepened with each time spent together. Without saying so, they had fallen in love, and each was as sure about that as if they *had* spoken about it. The only reason they didn't use those words was because he still had to concentrate on the game. But they knew their feelings, and trusted them, and were anxious for the time when they could say all the things they wanted to say without the tensions of the championship games overlying everything.

Los Angeles took the fifth game, 124–99. The defeat was crushing to the Pisces. Only Moses was used to the pressure in the first place, and now the others, having withstood pressure through the last weeks of the regular season and the first two rounds of the playoffs, felt themselves—now down 3–2 in the finals—crumbling under the greatest pressure of all.

"Observe!" Mona directed them in the locker room before the sixth game. The monitor showed video replays of their mistakes and lack of concentration in the fifth game.

All the Players studied their charts now with much more concentration and faith. Thus prepared, they went out and won the sixth game in Los Angeles, to even the series at 3–3. Jabbar suffered a mildly strained ankle in the fourth quarter, and without him, the Pisces slipped by to a 113–110 victory.

Toby and Moses spent the day between that game and the final one together, taking a riverboat cruise on the "Gateway Clipper." They stood at the rail, savoring the air that came from the confluence of the three rivers—Ohio, Allegheny, and Monongahela—that met at the "Golden Triangle" where the city of Pittsburgh lay.

"Welcome aboard my used-to-be-secret hiding place, lady," Moses said, gazing reflectively out over the landscape. "Been coming here for a long time. You know, to think things out, be alone."

She snuggled up to him playfully. "If I didn't know better, I couldn't imagine you ever wanting to be alone—without a crowd cheering for you. I mean, you're such a standout, and the crowds come to games largely to see—"

"C'mon, baby, don't make it harder for me." He smiled and patted her back. "What I'm trying to say is I *never* want to be alone. I mean, not really alone. You can be alone in front of a crowd—know what I mean? But what I'm trying to say is, I don't want to be alone, don't want to be without you. I mean . . ." he shook his head and laughed, "am I making any sense?"

"Nope," she said, teasing. Then she took his hands in hers and looked up into his eyes, a wry smile on her face. "Moses Guthrie, you gettin' sentimental on me?"

He pulled her close and hugged her. "Something like that, I guess. Just like that."

She held him tight. "Well, I guess I like that. I guess I *love* that."

He closed his eyes and kissed the top of her head, his smile suddenly gone. "I love you, Toby. I love you enough to marry you, if you don't think I'm crazy."

"You asking?"

"Yes."

"Yes."

"You answering?"

"Yes I am, Moses, oh yes. Oh Moses!" She pulled away, blinking. "Oh wow, you got me flyin'! Whoo! I gotta get back down to earth—let me think . . ."

"What you got to think about?"

Her eyes glistened. "About *us*, Moses. You know, I want to do it. I just . . . I just want it to be right."

He took her hands. "Take your time, little girl. 'Cause I'm right with you. I ain't goin' nowhere." He pulled her close. "Besides, we still got to beat L.A. I wouldn't want you marrying a loser."

Now the scene was set for the climactic game in the Pittsburgh Civic Arena. There was no doubt that the arena would be jammed to the rafters—had there been rafters in the magnificently domed arena. All 16,548 seats had been sold, plus an additional unreleased number for standees. And the scene inside the arena was unusual, even for a final game for the N.B.A. championship.

Added to the new, shiny plastic paint on the hardwood floors were, at either end, large pink-and-aqua paintings of the same fish that the Pisces had on their jerseys. And two more huge fish swam in a surrealistic, painted sea around the center jump circle.

Early fans waved banners that said "Fish power" and "Fish Fever." A group of Rev. Jackson's congregation seated in a special section brandished fish-shaped fans (combining Pisces with the influence of Mona's garb) and at the end of cheers, they leaped to their feet to holler "Amen!"

A stern-faced group in another section wore Arab headwraps and held up signs that said, "Truth Saves!"

Running Hawk fans wore headbands with single feathers sticking up from the back. One sitting in their midst had a huge tom-tom with which he accented their chants.

And throughout the arena people munched not hot dogs but "smelt dogs," hot-dog rolls wrapped around the tiny silver lake fish with tartar sauce instead of mustard.

Suddenly onto the court for the pre-game show came the new group of cheerleaders, the Fishsticks—men and women dressed in wild Pisces colors, mixing Mona's styles with funky disco styles, waving fans and kicking their silver sneakers high. They danced and boogied and swung their hips and kicked their feet around the arena, leading hand-clapping cheers. The men of the group hoisted the women high and spun them around, then went into intricate dance routines. One repeated cheer was: "Two, four, six, eight— What sign makes us operate? Pisces! Pisces! *Pisces!*"

Outside the arena, the streets, bridges, and sidewalks were already a hopeless tangle of strangled traffic. Cars, buses, motorcycles, bicycles, and skateboards all mashed together and deadlocked in a single aim that was shared by the entire city—to get to the Civic Arena for the championship game. Stranded drivers left their cars and hoofed it from wherever they were.

One black man, dressed in a mink coat, as was his lady, yanked the keys out of his '71 Chrysler Diplomat, jumped out, took her hand, and led her on the most direct route possible. That route happened to take them through the back seat of a Lincoln limousine occupied by a matron in a long gown and her escort in a tuxedo.

As these occupants gaped in disbelief, the couple ducked in one door, carefully avoided stepping on the seated couple's feet, and went out the other. En route the Brother tipped his hat to say, "Just passing through. May the fish be with you!"

People dressed in fish sweatshirts, fish beanies, carrying fish signs, and even small jars of swimming fish, made their way through the chaos to the arena.

Inside at the press table sat Marv Albert, the calm and controlled play-by-play man from New York, here to call the game over network TV.

" . . . Last Thursday night," he was saying into the mike and the camera, "we were there in Los Angeles for game six of the league finals. And I must say, it was a contest that was not always pretty basketball, not even *good* basketball. Twenty-two fouls were called in the first quarter alone. But in any case it was *exciting* basketball. And the Pisces evened up the series at three games apiece. And so here we are at the splendid Civic Arena in Pittsburgh, Pennsylvania, for game seven to decide the championship of the National Basketball Association. And here with us tonight to describe some of the tension surrounding the game, we have Pittsburgh's own Murray Sports, now in the L.A. locker room. Let's go downstairs. Murray, it's all yours."

"Thanks, Marv." The camera came in on Murray, who stood with a hulking and familiar member of the Lakers. "Right here with the new L.A. strongman—forward Lucian Tucker—recently signed by the Lakers after leaving the Pittsburgh team several weeks ago when it was still the Pythons." He thrust the mike at Tucker. "Lucian, I know you can feel it down here, all this pre-game tension so thick it's—"

"Thick like some sport hustler's fat tongue workin' overtime, Murray," Tucker said gruffly.

Behind them, the L.A. team, dressed in their dark blue uniforms, waited to go onto the floor, some of them watching the interview.

"Never did like you," Lucian continued, "even when I was playin' for Pittsburgh. You never wanted to talk to me then, so how come now?"

"Why, um, uh . . ." Murray looked around, perspiring, feeling Lucian's cold eyes on him. The TV minicam crew kept a tight focus on their two faces, excluding from the frame the crate Murray was standing on to put his head somewhere near Lucian's. " . . . That is—Lucian, that's all water under the bridge, okay? Right now, the key question for everybody is what's going on in your mind about tonight's game—the big one. The whole season comes down to this one, big game. If you could sum up your feelings in one word, what would it be?"

A slow, mean, toothy grin spread over Lucian's face. *"Revenge.* 'Cause I don't tolerate no astrology hocus-pocus at all. And I don't tolerate no Moses Guthrie makin' me look bad like he been doin'. That man has a bad habit of tryin' to cramp my *style,* so I'm gonna break him of that habit. I'm gonna stay on him like hot on ice—you dig? When he's tryin' to play his pretty perfume game, I'm gonna be there stinkin' him up—you dig? Same for the rest of them. Ain't no planets and magic gonna get in our way *tonight.* We gonna *gut* them fish!"

Lucian stalked away.

"Back to you, Marv," Murray said, and let out a long sigh of relief.

High above the arena floor in an enclosed passage-way, Halsey and Friesman followed a floor attendant around to the private lounge-type box reserved for Tilson Freight Lines. The attendant opened the door for them and stepped back.

Halsey slapped a ten-dollar bill into the young man's hand. "Just remember where you got that, kid."

Upon entering the plush box, they were greeted by an arena "Glad Gal," who presented them with a tray of drinks from the bar. They each took a martini.

Friesman looked around, admiringly. "Very nice here. Better, I would say, than my club."

Halsey tasted his drink. "As I've always said, what's the point of wealth if you don't know how to enjoy it?" He took a longer swig. "And while we're on the subject of enjoyment, I wouldn't miss tonight's show for anything in the world. I'm trusting you for much of that, of course." He eyed the lawyer a bit threateningly.

"The world's yours, Mr. Tilson." Friesman gave him a confident smile.

"Not quite yet. But you see before you a man that's only two hours away from everything he wants, every-thing he's *always* wanted—a restoration of the proper order of things." He chuckled as he gazed down on the court below. "Oh my yes—nothing like an old-time fish fry to put things right."

8

The arena was near bursting with the crowd—much more than official capacity. And nobody was sitting down.

"Ladies and gentlemen!" boomed the P.A. "The Los Angeles Lakers!"

From the tunnel and onto the floor came the Lakers, a juggernaut of power and size. They charged out confidently, angrily, and were greeted by a swell of hisses and boos. They responded by going into an intimidating demonstration of slam dunks. When that had somewhat quieted the partisan crowd, they relaxed a bit and began taking jumpshots from around the hoop at their end of the floor.

The dancing Fishsticks did their best to diminish the menace of the Lakers, prancing this way and that along the sidelines, waggling their outstretched arms and chanting voodoo.

From the retirement-home section at the other end of the court, the geriatric contingent, wearing fish beanies, booed and gave Bronx cheers and banged their canes on the floor.

While the crowd settled down in anticipation of the entry of their beloved Pisces, Ola and Brandy, up in the high balcony seats, held hands nervously. In the seats over the tunnel, Mike and Michelle sat silently, leaning together and also holding hands.

Mike looked around at the awesome crowd. "Couldn'ta stuck another body in here anywhere, unless they opened the dome and stacked 'em up through it."

In another part of the city, Mona emerged from her storefront entrance, clutching her silver strongbox. It was dark and quiet as she approached the open door of her silver limousine. She started to step in when she noticed that the back seat was empty, her regular guard was not there.

Immediately she was grabbed from the rear by a huge man who stepped from the shadows. He clamped a hand harshly over her mouth, shoved her into the rear seat, jumped in behind her, and slammed the door.

"Go!" the man shouted. The limo sped off into the night.

Mona, as confused as she was dazed and scared, was pushed onto the floor and held down by the knee of one of the goons. She could not see the driver. But she could see the one looming over her, with his leering smile and his teeth glinting from the passing streetlights. She was pressed up against the folded jumpseats, powerless and frightened.

Back at the arena, the crowd was growing impatient for the entrance of the Pisces. People checked their watches and looked toward the tunnel.

L.A. finished their warm-ups, climaxed by Lucian Tucker's savage dunk that almost ripped the net off. As they went to their bench, the crowd greeted them with renewed boos that seemed to make them only prouder and more confident.

The booing could be heard even in the interior corridor near the locker rooms. Murray Sports led his mini-cam crew up to the door of the Pisces room, babbling into the mike.

"No doubt about it, folks, it's going to be a hot one in Steel City tonight. You can almost feel the heat from the Pisces locker room." He put his hand on the door. "Now we will give you a last peek at your favorites just before they take the floor to . . ." he pushed the door open, "play . . ."

He froze as his eyes and the camera fixed on an empty room. Not a sign of any Pisces.

"Well . . . okay . . . back upstairs to you, Marv."

Owner H. Sander Tilson approached the private section behind the scorer's table, where the league commissioner, a bespectacled, conservatively dressed man in a blue suit and button-down blue shirt, sat. Cantrell followed Tilson, tossing down a couple of Bromos.

Tilson was tickled literally pink, his face glowing, as he took a seat beside the commissioner. He signaled behind him, and up came a portly vendor toting a portable helium tank in one hand and a fistful of pink balloons in the other. The vendor puffed up a balloon and handed it to Tilson.

Inflated, the balloon was a fish, and Tilson presented it to the commissioner with the importance of giving him a plaque. "With my compliments, Commissioner —my symbol."

The Commissioner took the balloon, cleared his throat uneasily as he pondered what to do with it, then put it in his lap and gave Tilson a sincere look —not noticing that the balloon floated up and away.

"Mr. Tilson, I cannot commend you enough for what you've done for basketball." He looked around. "This crowd, this spirit, this game—Sir, you've put some *zip* back into the N.B.A.!"

A man at peace with his universe, Tilson basked in the praise and the expectant murmuring of the huge crowd and the beauty of the repainted court. He kicked off his shoes, propped his feet up on the seat in front of him, and smiled contentedly.

The P.A. system rasped, then produced the voice of the announcer. "And now, ladies and gentlemen! From the skies—the Pittsburgh *Pisces!*"

Tilson nudged the commissioner. "Fasten your seat belt, sir," he said gleefully. "It's show time!"

The lights dimmed and a hush fell over the arena. There was a muffled creaking and sliding as the dome opened slowly, like the petals of a night-blooming flower, exposing a widening and spectacular view of the moonlit sky.

The crowd emitted a loud, collective gasp.

Searchlights lit up the sky. And into the lights drifted a huge hot-air balloon, its panels colored pink and aqua, its large gondola a silvery, scaled, finned model of a fish that reflected the lights like a multi-faceted mirror. As it descended toward the opened dome, members of the Pisces team could be seen leaning over the edge of the gondola, waving at the crowd below.

Suddenly a loud disco tune blared from somewhere in the arena, and the Fishsticks, lit by flashing laser beams, took to the center of the court and began performing a wild, exuberant dance of welcome around a circular platform that had been rolled onto the center jump circle.

As the audience roared and stomped and clapped, the balloon descended through the dome and came to a soft landing on the platform.

Suddenly, the house lights came up full. To thunderous applause and cheers, the Pisces stepped proudly from the gondola and trotted gloriously over to their bench, the ovation and hurrahs of the fans and the bouncy rhythms of the music reverberating all around them. The dome closed over the scene.

Arriving from the locker room area, Tyrone and Rudy paused to watch the balloon's descent and landing, then hurried to the Pisces bench. Tyrone's face had a worried expression.

"I don't like this," he said to Rudy. "Mona's forty-five minutes late already. And she's *never* been late before."

"Maybe she got stuck in traffic like everybody else."

"Nope, not Mona. She woulda got here, just like *we* got here."

"Yeah, she's one of the team." Rudy suddenly looked worried too. "Think anything's happened, Tyrone?"

"Well, we can only hope she's got a reason. Mona's generally in control of things."

"Yeah, let's hope so."

Mona was not in control—not at all. The limo in which she was prisoner was headed away from the city, zooming through the deserted streets of the suburbs. She was still on the floor, gazing up into the square, unshaven face of the goon who rested a foot lightly on her neck to make sure she didn't try anything.

"Sir," she said, smiling bravely, "mind if I clear my throat?"

He took a puff on his cigarette, the embers of the tip glowing in the dark, as he pondered the request. "Yeah, okay. So clear yer throat. Just stow the gab."

He lifted his foot. She took a deep breath and let out an ear-splitting scream.

The goon quickly slapped his foot down again on her neck, choking her.

"Hey!" cried the driver, half-turning around. "What's goin' on back there?"

"Guess she had somethin' stupid to say," said the goon in the back seat casually. "So I had somethin' smart to do, which was shut her up."

"Keep her that way."

"Don't worry."

Mona could scarcely breathe.

The Pisces bench was tense. Brockington paced around rubbing his hands as the team took off their warm-up suits. Players glanced often at Mona's empty seat, and muttered to each other. But nobody was anxious to ask the obvious question.

Setshot was not so inhibited. "Hey, Tyrone, how come Mona's not here?"

Tyrone just shook his head dejectedly.

Rev. Jackson faced up toward the dome, closed his eyes, and raised his arms. "Lord, give us a sign!"

Then he opened his eyes and looked at his teammates. "Well, all we got's our *own* sign—no sign of her. But somethin' fishy's sure goin' on. Boys, the *Devil* is loose tonight. As the French would say, 'Mon Dieu, Mon Dieu,' and as we would say, no Mondieu."

Truth looked his very sternest. "I dig where you're comin' from, Rev. We're missin' our fox and without her we're in a fix. Maybe we shouldn't have messed around up there with that balloon. Maybe the planets got confused."

Driftwood took off his headphones sadly. "No Mona, no magic. My stomach's upset." He put a hand over his belly. "I don't like unpleasantness."

Shoulder to shoulder, the twins kept trying to smile and see the brighter side of things.

"Well," Benny said, "my momma had this friend from Jamaica who had this saying . . ."

"Bettah mos' come, mon," Kenny finished.

"The only 'bettah' thing that could come would be Mona," Running Hawk said. "Everything else is nothing." Then he went into a soft, monotone Indian chant.

"What's that mean?" Setshot asked.

"It means, somebody help us through the night—I think."

Jackhammer sidled up to Moses. "I mean, without our queen, how we gonna make the scene?"

Moses shrugged. He glanced over to the seats behind the bench to see Toby, who waved. Moses did not wave back. He was lost in his own thoughts. The significance of Mona's absence was as obvious to him as anybody else, but there was also a game to play, with her or without her. And without her, Moses would have to carry the team even more than usual. He was not going to moan or sulk about it. So he concentrated on his job for the evening, which was to play basketball better that he had ever played in his life.

The warning buzzer sounded, and the teams gathered around their coaches. The Pisces looked at the floor as Brockington addressed them.

"Okay, okay," he said peppily, "so we don't have Mona. But, well, uh—hey! At least we've got her *chair!* That's something, huh? And we have our game plan. Yessir, team execution's the key."

The Pisces responded with moody stares, either at him or at their feet.

"Come on, guys, it's like whoever it was said— think big, *win* big!" He blinked several times. "Right? Huh?" He got no answers at all. He looked over at the L.A. bench and was appalled at the difference. The Lakers were stalking around impatiently, looking at the Pisces, snarling and grunting, looking more ready to play than any team he had ever seen.

"Oh well . . ." He tried to rally them by patting a

few of them on the back. "Okay. Game time. Right. You know what they say, gang—there's no tomorrow tonight."

"Yeah," Running Hawk spat, "and there ain't no tonight today, Coach, if Mona don't show."

"Knock that stuff off, men," Moses said softly but firmly. "We play no matter what. We give it what we got." He gave Tyrone a faint smile of reassurance.

"He's right," Brockington said. "Mona or no, it's time to do or die. So let's get out there and play some ball. Shoot! Pass! Execute! I'll handle the time-outs and substitutions." He straightened his tie. "I'll be here if you need me."

The players leaned together and slapped palms half-heartedly, then the starting five of Moses, Jackson, Setshot, Bullet, and Driftwood shuffled out to center court—from which the balloon and now the glow of hope had been removed.

They lined up, the referee tossed the ball high between the centers, and the game was on.

Kareem controlled the tip. Guard Norm Nixon dribbled the ball into the forecourt and lobbed it in to Kareem. The towering center backed in on Jackson and turned for the sky-hook. Two points for L.A.

The Pisces brought the ball up, lost it immediately, and L.A. scored again on a fast break.

Toby, in a seat just behind Mona's empty one, leaned down to Tyrone. "Little Bro, my intuition's telling me something's really wrong." She tapped the empty seatback. "I can feel it."

"Yeah, sis." His eyes were downcast. "I feel it too. But what can anybody do? What can *I* do?"

"Feeling responsible, huh?"

"Sort of, I guess. Since I got the whole business started with her, everybody's leaning on her."

L.A. scored again.

Toby sat thinking. "Hey, Tyrone!"

"Yeah?" He turned to her.

"You started it, all right. But you didn't start it blind. You knew something about it. You knew a whole lot! The charts!"

"Huh?"

"The charts, Tyrone! You did them before you ever found Mona. So maybe . . ."

Tyrone sprang to his feet, snapping his fingers. "The charts! You just said somethin', Toby! You're right! Maybe I can do 'em!"

Then his smile fell. "But geez, I don't know . . . I was only playin' around then, and—"

She smacked his shoulder. "Tyrone, you're about to make yourself some of your own breaks. You got what it takes, little bro. Go!"

He pinched his lips together, gritted his teeth, clenched his hands, spun, and raced down the side-lines and disappeared into the tunnel.

High up in the sanctum of the Freight Lines private lounge, Halsey and Friesman watched the game through the tinted glass. In front of them was also a TV monitor bringing them the play-by-play over the network.

" . . . And again L.A. takes advantage of yet another Pisces turnover," Albert was saying, "the seventh such lapse by Pittsburgh—and now it's a three-on-one fast break led by Nixon . . . the pass off, and score! Turnovers are killing the Pisces right now . . ."

Smugly satisfied, Halsey's eyes glittered with a fiercely happy intensity as he watched the game below him and the monitor in front. He swabbed at his moist neck with a paisley handkerchief. "I love it! Love it! Friesman, take a memo."

Friesman reached for his yellow legal pad.

"I want the home addresses of those L.A. boys after the big win. We want to send them something really nice and appropriate."

"For the entire Laker—"

"No, you jury-rigging old fool!"

"Oh, yes, I see." He was nudged gently and looked up to see a Glad Gal offering him another drink.

"Write it down!"

"Yes sir, yes sir. I have it, Mr. Tilson. Dinner for two. Good?"

"Perfect! Make it some fine place with a good view —where longshoremen like them prefer to dine."

Moses had the ball in his forecourt. He faked left,

drawing Lucian Tucker that way, then spun off to his right, drove, leaped, and twisted in mid-air to score.

Hustling back upcourt after the basket, Tucker elbowed Moses hard as he rushed past. The two exchanged unmistakably hostile looks.

The L.A. offense moved with precision. Kareem set a pick and Tucker drove off it for a lay-up.

On the next time down the court, Setshot was fouled as he tried a long shot, and he made both free throws.

But L.A. scored two more quick baskets.

The game was clearly getting away from the Pisces.

Tyrone, down in the locker room, was busier than he had ever been in his life. Books and chart forms were spread all over the floor around him, and he was on his hands and knees furiously scribbling numbers and symbols on other pieces of paper. From time to time he slapped his forehead in frustration.

From the overhead monitor came the voice of Marv Albert. ". . . Ten already for Jabbar, eight for Nixon, eight for Tucker. Moses has eleven for the Pisces, but they seem unable to get any kind of fluid game together on either offense or defense. Pisces Coach Brockington is substituting freely, obviously looking for the combination that will settle them down and get some of that old—or rather new—Pisces magic back in their game. The Lakers show no signs of letting up . . ."

Bitter and defeated, Tyrone finally threw down his pencil and sat back on his haunches. Then angrily he began crawling through the mass of papers and ripped them up, scattering the pieces wildly. He got up and stormed over to the lockers and beat his fists against them, slamming them loudly with nobody but himself to hear. Then he collapsed beside a bench, tears flooding his face.

"Oh, Mona, I can't do it. . . . We need you so bad. . . . I can't do it alone . . ."

His pathetic wails echoed in the empty locker room.

The limousine bearing Mona glided down the empty highway like a silver phantom.

The goons were laughing and passing a giant-sized

can of beer back and forth. The goon in the back eyed Mona, who was on the floor with a wide piece of tape plastered over her mouth. She was sitting up now, leaning against one of the folded jump seats. Her eyes were angry and staring.

"So, you wanna know where we're takin' ya, princess?" the man growled huskily. "Well, I ain't gonna tell ya where we're takin' ya." He paused dramatically and chuckled. "But if I wanted to tell ya, I'd tell ya this much—you got a one-way ticket, unnerstand?"

"Haw!" came from the driver. "Haw, haw, haw! You sure got a way with words, Crunch!"

The goon in the back burst into laughter of his own, spewing suds from his mouth. Then he crushed the half-filled can easily in his bear paw, spraying more foam and beer over the back seat and Mona's head. Squirming around on the floor to avoid the flood as much as she could, she issued gagged sounds of protest from behind her tape.

"Haw!"

"You wanna hear the game, princess? I'll turn it on for you." Crunch tuned in the rear-seat console, and the account she heard was anything but consoling.

Tyrone had finally spent his despair in the locker room. He dragged himself to his feet, wiped the remaining tears away, and sadly cleaned up the mess he had made. He was in no hurry. He was unable to hurry. He was in a kind of daze.

He left the locker room and slogged into the tunnel. He passed an elderly guard with a transistor radio at his ear.

"Too bad, Tyrone," the old man said, tapping his back. "Looks like our Cinderella team's about to turn into a pumpkin."

Tyrone nodded and continued on. Then abruptly he stopped and turned back. "What's that you said?"

"What I said? Just that the Cinderella team's about to change into a pumpkin, that's all—you know, like Cinderella's coach at midnight." He shook his head. "What a shame."

Tyrone stared at him, clenching and unclenching his

hands and mumbling, "Cinderella . . . midnight . . . pumpkin . . ." He stepped quickly back to the guard. "What time you got?"

The guard checked his watch. "About ten-ten. What difference does that make?"

Tyrone had already whirled away and was sprinting down the tunnel. "Lots!" he called back over his shoulder.

On the court, Kareem leaped to block a shot by Bullet, knocking the ball into Nixon's hands. Nixon hurled it upcourt to Carr, who raced in for the lay-up uncontested.

The crowd was miserable, and the best example of that was in the section at the end of the court, where the wheelchair men sat dejectedly. They slumped in their chairs, the fish-propellers on their beanies still.

"This isn't a game," said Sweets, his hand over his eyes, "it's a sacrifice."

"Rice?" said the man next to him, putting a listening horn to his ear. "What's rice got to do with this slaughter?"

"The whole night's wasted," Sweets said.

"Tasted? What's worse than the taste of *defeat?*"

Tyrone scurried up the sideline and slid on his knees the final few feet on the slick floor, coming to a stop at Toby's feet. "Toby! Toby! I got the answer!"

She looked around quickly, expecting to see Mona. "What answer you talking about? She's not here."

"I'm talkin' about the *solution!*" He waved at the court. "It's all wrong out there tonight—nothing's working!"

"I can *see* that. Everybody can see that."

"But *why?*"

"Because Mona's not here."

"No! Not just that! I mean, she would say the same thing, if she was here. It's because the Pisces are *blocked!*"

"Blocked?"

"All jammed up until tomorrow! I figured it out, but it took me a while to realize what I had, 'cause it didn't seem to make sense. Now it does. Nothin' can go right for them until tomorrow—which is exactly

. . ." he pushed up Toby's sleeve to expose her watch, "one hour and forty-five minutes from now. Ten-fifteen, right? One hour and forty-five minutes left of today. After that the planets change, their cusps and stuff. After midnight, Toby, we're home free!"

"Home free?"

"Untouchable. Tomorrow!" He beamed. "See, all we got to do is *stall!* All we gotta do is make this game end *tomorrow,* which means just any time after midnight!" He crawled up next to her and pulled her head down to whisper in her ear. "Now here's what we gotta do . . ."

The first half was drawing to a close—a blessed close as far as the Pisces were concerned, anything to give them a break in the horrific action.

Kareem slid across the key to loft in another skyhook.

Eight seconds were left. The Pisces brought the ball up quickly, looking for Moses. Tucker was covering him like a glove. Bullet sent up a long jumper that missed as the buzzer sounded.

The half ended with L.A. in the lead, 63–41.

The Pisces fled the court for the tunnel, hearing boos from the crowd behind them. By the time they reached their locker room, the team was at its nadir of dejection.

But Brockington, hot on their heels, asserted himself. "What is going on out there?" he barked at the sagging players. "No hustle, no bustle, no execution, no heart, no—"

"Chart!" Jackhammer put in, scowling. "Bring on Mondieu!"

"Well now, hey, you guys, listen up. There *is* no Mondieu!" Brockington wrung his hands. "We have to face the facts . . ."

"Face the facts is face the *acts.* And our acts is losin' while L.A.'s cruisin'."

"Okay, okay," Moses said, "we got work to do in here. Let's listen up like the coach says."

The players quieted and flopped down on the benches. Nobody looked up at the coach.

The Tilson Freight Lines V.I.P. box was aglow from

the monitor and the smiles of Halsey and Friesman. Halsey's eyes were focused on nothing particular, just wide and bright.

"Friesman, listen to me and improve your mind. Now, your basic slob might think we've just seen one half of a basketball game. Not entirely true." He flourished his arm grandly. "What we've actually witnessed is the natural restoration of proper order. The reason I know this to be true is the reason I'm up here, not down there with all the slobs and the hoi polloi, where my brother is."

Friesman nodded and reached for the big box of popcorn and stuffed a mass of it into his mouth.

Halsey slapped the back of his head, sending flecks of popcorn out of his mouth. "Friesman! Must you continually eat that junk in front of me like an ordinary boob in the cheap seats? I hired you for your brain, not your displays of junk-food addiction . Show some discipline, man! If you have to eat, eat brain food."

Friesman swallowed "Fish?"

Halsey slapped the back of his head again. "I banish that word from this box!"

Brockington puffed up his chest and paced back and forth in the locker room, holding up a pencil for his team to see. "See this?" He snapped it in half dramatically. "Now see this? Two halves. I'm throwing one away . . ." he tossed it off to the side, "and keeping the other." He held up the remaining half. "Notice that I've kept the half with the point on it and discarded the half with the eraser." He thrust out his jaw and resumed pacing. "Know what that means? One half gone, and that can't be *erased*. One half left, and that's the *point*. And with just the point left, and no eraser, we can't erase the mistakes we've already made, and we can't make any *more* mistakes!"

The players exchanged fatigued, hopeless looks.

"Tonight we have a chance to make history—"

"Later for the history," Jackhammer interjected, "just clear up the mystery."

"Forget the mystery! We deal with the *reality!* And the reality is that L.A. is wiping up the floor with us!" Brockington took a stumbling step backward surprised by the candor of his own words. "That is, um, clearly what I'm talking about is pulling a tough one out of the fire." He lowered his voice and spoke earnestly. "Guys, just remember, coming close doesn't count in basketball—close only counts in horseshoes and hand grenades."

"And team play," Moses put in. "Close counts there. We got to play together."

"Right! Moses is right!" Brockington nodded at the players and they nodded back—not with high spirit, but with some willingness to try, at least.

Tyrone had gathered together Ola and Brandy, along with a balloon vendor, in the storage area under the stands. He urgently whispered the outlines of his plan to them.

Brandy and Ola were perplexed. "But how we supposed to do that?" they asked together.

Tyrone gave them a knowing smile. For a few moments, they just stared at him. Then they nodded and smiled, too.

Tyrone pointed up to a nearby clock, showing 10:28. "All right, we got it to do. Let's go!"

They all slapped palms and hurried off in different directions.

The three game officials were in their dressing room, two of them stripped to their shorts and drying off with towels. Their uniforms were hung on a nearby door, airing out. They were debating a disputed call.

"I'm telling you," said one of them, "it was a bass-ackwards call!"

"Look!" snapped back the head ref. "I was in position to make the call—you weren't. So I called it. *Period!*" He looked over at the third official. "Where's those cokes?"

"Oh. Coming right up, chief." He trotted out of the room.

"You're saying I wasn't in position?" continued the other official. "It was my call, I had it, and it wasn't goal-tending."

"You were behind the board. I was out front. I had the view of the whole arc. It was goal-tending. And listen—that's done! This particular discussion is *over!*"

"Geez, guy can't even—"

"Gentlemen?" Brandy peeked in the door, two king-sized cokes in her hands. They looked quickly over. "Pardon the intrusion, sirs . . ." She stepped shyly in. ". . . But these are with the compliments of the management."

"Oh."

"Geez, thanks, but we sent out for—"

"Hi!" Ola breezed in.

"Uh, hello, ma'am." The head ref felt distinctly naked. "Hello to you both. Sorry we aren't—"

"What we were wondering about," Brandy said, cocking her head, "is that goal-tending call."

"See?" said the overruled official to the head ref.

"Sure looked bad to us," Ola said evenly.

"Looked bad!" The head ref sucked on his coke. "What're you talking about? Moses hit the ball on the way down. That's all there is to it."

"Sure looked like the shot was on the way up to me—to us," Ola said, "and to everybody else."

"What did I tell you?" said the assistant ref, smugly.

"You don't tell me anything!" the head ref spouted. "None of you."

Feeling vindicated, the other man lowered his voice and spoke reasonably. "I'm not trying to tell you anything. All I'm saying is it's a championship game, and the calls have to be right. Right, girls?"

"Right on!" they sang in unison.

"Hey, listen!" The head ref stepped among them, looking at his associate, chopping the air with his hand. "Never mind about the goal-tending. What about the hand-check calls you *haven't* been making? You still going by the old rules or something?"

"*Hand-check* calls?" The other official slapped his forehead. "There hasn't been any! Everybody's been keeping hands off!"

Brandy waved her hands. "Now hold on, wait a minute. What y'all talkin' about? Maybe y'all could explain this hand-check business to us and settle it that way. We neutral. Right, girl?"

Ola nodded soberly.

"So you want to know about hand-checking?" The

head ref grabbed her wrist. "Come here, watch, both of you."

Placing one hand on Brandy's hip, he demonstrated. *"This* is hand-checking if the dribbler's progress is impeded by your hand pushing on him this way. Got that?" He turned to the other official. *"You* got that?"

"Got it? I've been on top of it for years! I'm on the crew for this game, ain't I? The championship game?"

Pushing Brandy aside, the head ref went eyeball to eyeball with his associate, hands on his hips. "Yeah? Well, we'll see about that! Wait'll I make my report!"

"Oh yeah? Well, we *will* see about that! The commissioner's office will have the game films and—"

Brandy snatched one set of clothes from the door. "And we'll . . ."

Ola snatched the other set. "See ya later!"

They bolted from the room, laughing hysterically.

"Hey!"

"Our clothes!"

Meanwhile, in the L.A. locker room, the coach was fuming. He looked up at the clock, which showed 10:45. "Where are those lousy refs?" He banged on a locker. "Two minutes! We're already behind two minutes on the start of the second half. Unbelievable!"

The Lakers paced around nervously. They were as anxious to get back to the game as he was—to complete the rout and take home the championship.

"What kind of a crummy place *is* this, anyway?" the coach continued to rant. "Playing the final game on the road is tough enough, without this kind of nonsense! I give 'em thirty seconds more, then I'm going after 'em!"

Brockington also noted the time as he prowled back and forth in the Pisces locker room, snapping a towel in his hands. "A plot! Yeah, that's what this delay's all about!" He darted his eyes around. "Gonna check on the home addresses of those officials, where they grew up, where they went to school, where their aunts and uncles live. Probably all L.A."

His players were not as anxious as the Lakers. They were glad for the extra rest.

He peered at them and held his hands out, palms down. "But stay calm, men. Stay cool. They're just trying to rattle us, test our nerve. Well, we can handle pressure. Right, guys?"

"Yeah," Moses answered.

"But I tell you, another thirty seconds and I . . ."

Though the goons had taped Mona's mouth, they had not covered her eyes. And while they drove and drove and turned here and there, she could recognize certain landmarks that indicated to her that her kidnappers were taking not a direct route to some distant location, but rather a circuitous one that meandered through the outskirts and suburbs of the city without ever really getting far away from the metropolis. In fact, the goons themselves seemed to recognize that they weren't getting where they wanted to go.

"Hook a left," barked the goon with her in the back.

"Right."

"*Left,* I said, you gumbo!"

"I *am* goin' left, you gizzard-head!" He made a whining turn.

The goon with Mona grunted and burped. He flashed a toothy grin at her. "Don't you worry none, lady. When we get there, *you* get there to stay. And we ain't lost, so don't you worry about that. We're just makin' sure there ain't nobody tailin' us. Right, Bilbo?"

"Right it is, Crunch." He made a right turn.

The limousine bounced along on a rutted concrete lane. Mona jounced on the floor.

"Don't try'n talk, lady. Talk is cheap. This here's an expensive ride."

"Haw, Crunch! You said it! I'm countin' it already!"

"If you can count to three, that's how long I'm givin' you to get us headed in the right direction!"

"Don't holler at me, wimp, I'm the driver!"

Mona winced as the shocks from the rough road tumbled her around.

The L.A. coach barreled down the corridor, so angry he seemed to smoke from his ears. He was sideswiped by the fleeing Ola and Brandy. They tossed the officials' clothes in his face and sped on before he could say anything.

He was disentangling himself from the clothes, sputtering with rage, when he heard a "Pssst!" from behind the door to the refs' dressing room. The officials leaned out their door, hunched over in their underwear.

"Am I going *crazy?*" The coach put his hand over his eyes, then looked again. "Don't you jerks realize we've got a championship game to finish? Suit up! This ain't a high-diving competition!" He threw them their uniforms. "Here! I don't pretend to know what happened, all I know is we better get on that court in sixty seconds or I'll file a protest with the commissioner!"

The humiliated refs ducked back inside to get dressed.

As the L.A. players burst from the tunnel and onto the court, Albert and Murray at the press table nodded at each other.

Albert bent to the mike. "Well, fans, after what will undoubtedly be remembered as the longest halftime in play-off history, it seems that we're about ready to begin the second half. Los Angeles has just taken the court—and here come the Pisces . . ."

The crowd cheered for all it seemed worth, relieved at least that the Pisces had shown up—the fans hadn't forgotten how the Pisces had *not* shown up for the second half many weeks ago against Boston, when they were still the feckless Pythons.

Partly concealed near the mouth of the tunnel and huddled next to the two ball carts, Tyrone turned to the balloon vendor. "Okay," he said quietly, "roll out."

The vendor started pushing one cart, Tyrone got behind the other.

"You got 'em all done?" Tyrone asked as they headed for the court.

"Just squeezed out the last one, partner."

"Beautiful!" Tyrone saw the scoreboard clock: 10:52.

They rolled the ball racks innocently up to the scoring table. The tardy officials came hurriedly over.

The head ref grabbed a ball. "We gotta start right away! The TV people are going crazy!"

The ref started out toward the jump circle. He bounced the ball once, but it never came back to him. The ball took off, soaring up toward the top of the dome.

The crowd, not knowing whether it was part of the show or not, gaped at the ball until it became a dot against the huge surface of the dome.

"What the blazes is going on here?" the head ref shouted. "Will somebody give me a ball?"

Wanting to be helpful, Brockington trotted over and took another ball from the rack and pitched it out toward the ref.

But that ball didn't reach him either. It took off without even a bounce, flying to the roof to join the first. Then, released from the pressure against each other, the rest of the balls in the rack rose lazily, headed for the dome. Tyrone and the balloon vendor slapped palms.

The sound of laughter throughout the arena making him angrier by the second, the ref raced across the court to Brockington, grabbed the coach's tie, and yanked the taller man's face down to his level.

"Two minutes!" The ref yelled. *"Two* is all you got to get me a certified official N.B.A. basketball, Brockington! Any more of your messing around and I swear I'll either turn this over to the commissioner, or, or, or I'll personally eat your license to coach!"

Brockington sputtered and stammered and threw up his hands.

In the seats over the tunnel entrance, Mike and Michelle stared up at the balls nestled against the dome. Then Michelle looked down at the court. "Gee, Mike, if this goes on much longer I'll miss Gregory Peck on the 'Late Show'."

Mike grunted. "Don't blame me. I got nothin' to do with this."

"Yeah, but I mean, what's this stalling all about?"

"Stalling?"

"Yeah." She wrinkled up her nose. "It's like some-body doesn't want the game to begin or something."

"Stalling!" Mike's eyes opened wide. "The stars! Something!"

"What the heck are you—"

"Michelle! We've been married eleven years and that's the first intelligent thing you ever said. I love ya!" He gave her a quick peck on the cheek and jumped up.

"I'm not so sure I like what you just said about—"

He tossed her the binoculars. "I'll be right back, baby!"

"Back? Where you going?"

"Up!" He pointed to the top of the arena at a control platform suspended from the dome's center, atop the scoreboard.

"You gonna get the balls down?"

"Nope. Up there, though, that's where I'm goin'! Just keep your sweet eyes glued to where I'm pointing, sweetheart, and watch your man in the kind of action he's trained to do!"

"You gonna tighten something up there or—"

"Power to the Fish!" And with that, Mike took off running, bounding up the stairs to a service door at the top of the stands, leaving Michelle gaping and mystified.

9

A proper ball was found, and the second half began. It began right where the first half left off, with L.A. dominating. It was luck—just the normal kind—that kept the Lakers from blowing it open completely. They missed a few shots, committed a few turnovers, bungled some defensive maneuvers. The Pisces hung on with some forced shots that fell good, some fortunate calls from the refs, and the presence of Moses Guthrie.

Mike, meanwhile, was working his way up through the closed-off section behind the stands. He knew the section like the back of his hand. As the third quarter wore on, and the groans of the crowd reached his ears, he finally stepped onto the catwalk leading to the apex of the dome.

He was excited with his mission. He knew nothing of the Pisces' specific plight, but he had been following the papers enough to know that strange things guided his team, and was smart enough to suppose that the odd events and delays had something to do with those strange things—especially when combined with the fact that the star lady was not there and the Pisces were clearly not playing their game. It was obvious that, for some reason, they needed time. And they needed Mike.

As he climbed, Michelle fiddled with the focus wheel on the binoculars, keeping them trained where Mike had pointed, waiting for a sign from her husband that would indicate what in blazes he was doing. This was the most excitement she had had in months.

Mike slipped out of the hatchway and scrambled down onto the hanging platform from which the giant, round, hollow scoreboard was suspended. He paused to stare down at the seats, scanning the antlike mass of spectators for Michelle.

Michelle spotted him first. Holding the binoculars tight to her eyes with one hand, she waved with the other. "Mike-ee! Yoo-hoo! Hi, Mike-ee!"

From his position 150 feet above, Mike caught sight of her, yanked a white handkerchief out of his pocket and waved it over his head. "Mee-chelle! Here I am! I love ya, honey!" Neither could hear the other. Mike blew her a kiss. Entirely thrilled, bouncing up and down in her seat, Michelle blew several kisses back up to Mike.

Mike went to work, adrenalin coursing through him. He reached into the breaker box for the controls that could override those in the floor booth—controls for positioning the scoreboard. He pushed the "down" button, and, with him aboard, the scoreboard began its slow descent toward the floor below. Waving his handkerchief, he hollered like a rodeo rider, "Ya-hoo!"

The game continued. The Lakers scored, and then applied a full-court press as the Pisces tried to bring the ball up. Trapped in the backcourt, Truth passed up to Driftwood near the center line. But Tucker had reacted on defense and was on Driftwood quickly, knocking the ball loose. They both battled for the ball, and both ended up on the floor with their arms wrapped around it. The ref whistled and held his thumbs up, calling for a jump ball.

The tired players took their time lining up at the center circle for the jump. All were oblivious to what was descending above them.

But gradually the crowd was becoming aware. Beginning from the highest seats and spreading downward, the spectators began to rise and gasp and gawk at the lowering scoreboard.

Holding the ball out on his palm, the ref set it up between Driftwood and Tucker. The ball went up, their eyes went up, and they saw it.

Too late. With a thump, the hollow scoreboard dropped around them, sealing them inside.

The crowd, stunned at first, and still confused, nonetheless clapped and whistled and cheered and stomped —it was, at the least, a good show. From the top of the scoreboard, Mike acknowledged them with upraised arms. From inside the board came the muffled voices of the ref, Driftwood, and Tucker.

"What is this?" came the ref's irate voice. "Get this apparatus *up!*"

"Get me outta here!" screeched Tucker, who was claustrophobic, and banged on the walls.

Driftwood's voice was softer, filled more with wonder than anything else. "A handball court for midgets maybe . . ."

Both benches quickly emptied, the players and coaches gathering around the scoreboard in bewilderment.

The second ref pushed his way through to the board. "Hey, Spiderman!" he yelled up at Mike. "What do you think you're doing?"

"Relax, pal, I'm with the City." Mike looked down casually. "Just running an annual safety check on your scoreboard here. No big deal." He seemed to be checking the switchbox.

"No big deal!" The ref waved his arms up and down as if trying to fly. "Move it up *pronto* or I'm gonna give this game to L.A. on a *forfeit!* You got that?"

Mike saluted. "Loud and clear, ace. Only take a few minutes." He fiddled with the switches.

Down at the end of the floor, Sweets swung his wheelchair around to face his friend. "Hey, you know what, Robbins?"

"What'cha say?" Robbins said, bringing up his earhorn.

"I'm dying to take Nurse Nix to the Wheelers' Ball."

"Stall? That what they're trying to do out there?"

That hadn't dawned on Sweets. Now it did. "Hey, you got something!"

"Bumping is right! Great idea! Let's do it!" He reached for the lever to start his motorized chair. "Sweets, it's time for us men to stand up and be counted!"

"Stand up?" Sweets scratched his head.

"Right. Band up, you and me!"

Mike was manipulating the controls on the board, causing it to rise a bit, then sink to the floor again, scattering the onlookers. He shook his head in mock discouragement. "Almost got her that time."

"You got sixty seconds," the ref called, looking at his watch.

"I'll do her." Counting down the seconds to himself, Mike finally raised the board when a minute was almost gone, and took it back aloft. He hoped he had accomplished something.

Players and officials regathered on the court and lined up for the center jump.

On the Pisces bench, Tyrone watched the clock as it ticked by 11:13. He was very anxious and barely hopeful. Just till midnight, if they could just make it till then . . .

Sweets and Robbins had their wheelchairs poised at the top of the ramp leading to the court. Robbins had a police whistle between his teeth.

"Okay, men," he said to Sweets, "hit the beach! No prisoners!"

Just as the ball went up for the jump, Sweets and Robbins exploded onto the court, wheelchairs humming at full throttle. They whizzed into the center circle, scattering players like ten-pins. Shrieking with delight, the duo closed on their primary objective— Lucian Tucker. They chased him downcourt to the basket and sideswiped him, forcing him to jump up and hang onto the rim to elude them.

Game officials and security guards gave chase as the wheelchairs zig-zagged back up the court. Sweets and Robbins swerved and wove their way among the grasping hands, cackling wildly, the propellors on their fish beanies spinning furiously.

As they dodged several lunges from the guards, the crowd began to shout "Ole!"

Soon other wheelchairs were on the court. And soon after that some skateboards joined them, then some people on rollerskates. General mayhem swept the Civic Arena.

Everybody seemed involved in either running, sliding, wheeling, or cheering. All except Tyrone. He sat stiffly on the bench, allowing himself only a thin smile, as he watched the minutes tick by on the clock.

The limousine was on a deserted dirt road when it got a flat tire. The two goons got out and jacked up the left rear wheel, then began arguing about which of them was actually to do the dirty work.

"Me?" said one. "I'm the *driver!* That's my specialty. I got my rights."

The other goon produced a lug wrench from the trunk and waved it menacingly. "And *this* is *my* specialty, numb-nose! How'd you like the right to have your head split open?"

In the back seat, Mona, her mouth still taped and now with her hands trussed up over her head, lashed to the passenger strap with a necktie, wiggled like a contortionist.

". . . Unbelievable!" came Albert's voice over the radio. "There almost appears to have been some kind of, well, perhaps *understanding* here in the arena to stall for time. It is already almost eleven-thirty, and we're barely into the fourth quarter. A relentless Los Angeles team has built an 84–70 lead, and we can only hope that order will be restored soon and the game resumed. Whenever that is, the Pisces will need all the help they can get to turn this around . . ."

Mona wrestled and squirmed. Her bonds were not all that secure—she had been tied only enough to keep her still while they watched her. But they were not watching her now. At last she pulled her hands free and stripped the tape from her mouth. She sat still for a moment, listening to the men outside.

By now the goons had removed the spare tire from the trunk, only to find it as flat as the one they meant to replace.

"Where'd you get yer license," barked one, "at a

garage sale? Some pro driver *you* are! Goin' off on a snatch job with no air in yer spare!"

"Car was supposed to be ready," the driver said sulkily. "I ain't supposed to be no mechanic."

"I had enough of you!" With that, he picked up the lug wrench again.

The driver picked up a hubcap to defend himself, using it as a shield. And they went at it. Sparks flew from the hubcap as the wrench clanked off it again and again.

Mona seized the opportunity to wriggle through the sliding glass partition into the front seat. As the fight continued outside, she huddled behind the wheel and checked the gauges and mechanisms. "Wheel . . . brakes . . . gas . . . keys . . . *go!*"

She slammed the car into gear and put the accelerator to the floor.

The drive wheel on the ground spun wildly, biting into the gravel and finally catching enough grip to pull the other wheel off the jack. The rear end slammed down and the car took off like a rocket, fishtailing on its flat tire and disappearing from the warring goons in a cloud of smoke and dirt.

Under the best of circumstances, Mona was not the world's best driver. She fought to keep control of the careening, flat-tired vehicle as it roared down the road. She stared ahead, goggle-eyed, her hands clamped to the wheel. "Hold on, Pisces, I'm coming! Mona's coming. Oh my stars!" She maneuvered past an oncoming bus, slid around a corner, bounced off a sidewalk, and continued on.

Back at the arena, the chaos continued, though the guards and officials seemed gradually to be gaining the upper hand, steering some of the wheelchairs off the court and chasing the skateboarders back up into the stands.

But the commissioner was indignant. "As God is my witness, sir," he barked at H. Sander Tilson, "this, this *outrage* has gone far enough!" He waved his arms angrily toward the court. "So listen to me, Tilson. I want this game finished immediately, or it's your *franchise!*"

Tilson was not really hearing. He was on a wave-length of his own, and while not understanding what lay behind all the furor on the court, was enjoying it immensely. It was *fun.* "Fantastic, commissioner! Isn't it all so marvelous? A night of endless magic! This is the way it should be all the time, don't you think? Basketball is a *game,* after all. Oh my, I can't *wait* to see what happens next!" He clapped his hands de-lightedly.

"Cantrell!" The commissioner turned back to the general manager, who sat numbly transfixed by the disaster. "I trust you will pass on my warning to the owner, when he *awakens!*" Cantrell reached for a Bromo.

Up in the private lounge, Halsey was as displeased as the commissioner. He fanned himself with his silk handkerchief as he paced back and forth, occasionally snarling down at the court. "Friesman, what this world needs is more handcuffs!" He flung a hand in the direction of the melee. *"Insanity* is what we're witness-ing here, the rabble running amok! The crazies taking over the asylum! The riffraff running the shop!"

"But, sir," Friesman eyed him nervously, "we're *winning.* Isn't that sufficient?"

"Sufficient! You ignoramus! Sufficient is enough. Enough is enough. This spectacle's more than enough! Chaos and commotion is loose down there, just like in the rest of the world, threatening all sane people rep-resented by *me!* It needs to be stamped out! And I'm the one to do the stamping!"

"Anything you would like me to—"

"Sit! That's what. Sit, or I'll stamp *you* out like an old campfire, you wimp! Out of my way!"

Friesman watched in frozen silence as Halsey bolted from the box and headed for the court.

For Tyrone, the last embers of hope were dying out. Normalcy had been restored to the court and the game was set to resume. The clock read 11:25—not a whole lot of time left until midnight, but enough to shatter his dreams.

"Just not gonna make it," he mumbled, burying his face in his hands.

The players gathered at their benches prior to going back out. The Pisces slumped down, already defeated and ready to quit—except Moses.

He stood tall in front of them, hands on his hips, glaring down. "Look at you!" he snarled at them uncharacteristically. They all looked up. "After all we been through together—all the struggles and work and wins to get here, is this all you guys got left?"

They hung their heads. Moses walked along the bench.

"Setshot!"

Setshot's head popped up.

"For years you dreamed of playing basketball somewhere. And here you are not only playing, but in the N.B.A. championship game! You going to roll over and die?" He walked further along. "Truth! You been on the receiving end of every bad deal in the deck, and you hung in long enough to get here. You gonna fold now and throw in your hand? And the Righteous Reverend Grady Jackson! You spent a lifetime preachin' on people, tellin' them how to cope from way up in your pulpit. Whether you were sincere or not is *your* business. But now you're down here in the congregation, and you got problems. You gonna cope or you gonna quit?"

Moses stepped back and eyed them all. "I can't speak for you people, but my momma raised me to be *ready*. You know what that means? She wanted me to be able to take it as it comes, whatever it is, whenever it comes. To stand up to any test that comes along. And I can speak for myself. I'm ready!"

He watched them, sensing an encouraging rustle among them. "I know what you're thinking. Well, astrology's only a mirror. So work it out. I worked it out and I like what I see. And *I'm* goin' back out on that court! I'm goin' out there to do what I got to do. Anybody comin' with me is comin' *now!*"

He turned his back to them and strode majestically onto the floor.

Rev. Jackson looked out at Moses standing alone among the Lakers. Slowly he rose from the bench. "Well," he said quietly, "I don't know how else to put it. But what we got to do is—all of us—is . . ." he raised his voice and sang out, as he raised his arms, *"rise like Lazarus!"* And he followed Moses onto the court.

And then the whole team got up, slapped palms all around, and the rest of the starting five trotted out to slap palms with Moses and Jackson.

The Fishsticks quickly formed their group along the sideline and roused the crowd with a Pisces cheer.

Appearing like a spear out of the night, the limo zoomed down the ramp onto the concrete area surrounding the arena. Fighting the wheel, Mona tried to control the skidding car. She hit the brakes, locking them and sending the car into a screeching slide. Guards scattered in panic as the car spun around and around and came to a halt two feet from the entrance door.

Shaken but resolute, Mona sprang out of the door, clutching her silver box. For a moment she was dizzy, and leaned over the hood. Then, swirling her cape behind her, she dashed into the arena.

She popped through the door like an out-of-control ice skater, slipped on the hem of her cape, flopped face down, and skidded onto the court in a belly slide that ended up under the Pisces basket—bringing the game to an abrupt halt just as it had finally got underway.

The fans recognized her immediately and sent up a whoop of joy. The Fishsticks went into a wild dance and led the crowd in the chant of "MO-NA! MO-NA! . . ."

Tyrone bounced off the bench, adding his cries to the welcome. The Pisces, led by Rev. Jackson, rushed over to her. She lay like a rag doll, her chiffon and lace costume spread around her and her cape covering her head.

"Easy now, Mondieu," the Reverend said, reaching down to help her. "Everything's under control."

She pulled herself up, smoothed her gown, tossed her cape behind her, and patted her flowing locks. "Of course," she said calmly, smiling. "Thank you."

She curtsied, then dismissed the resurrected team with a gentle wave of her hand. "Back to the game, men. I would just say that . . ." she nodded up at the clock, now showing 11:33, "tomorrow's a brand-new day. But now, go ahead, you've got work to do."

She took her accustomed seat, amid the cheers from the crowd, and the ball was put back in play.

But Halsey was ignorant of all this. He was blinded by his own inner rage and sense of disorder. He pushed and elbowed his way through the crowd, clawing to open his tie that was gagging him. " . . . All out of control! . . . People, planets, the synchrosity of the universe! *My* universe!" He discarded the tie into the crowd. "Don't you rabble realize that? *Calamity!*"

He charged onto the court like a mad elephant.

Tyrone had been tending to Mona. "Sure you're all right? Maybe you oughta go in and lie down."

"Nope." She had spotted Halsey. "I want to be on my feet for this one!"

Halsey was in the middle of the court, pulling at Lucian Tucker's jersey and railing at him. "Can't you *understand?* We have to restore order!"

"What the . . ."

"The natural scheme of things is in danger of being overthrown by a rabid pack of *fish!*"

In the stands, Tilson never moved from his comfortable position. He smiled contentedly and elbowed the commissioner. "Look at that! How nice! My brother's finally having some fun!"

The commissioner buried his face in his hands.

Halsey dropped to his knees and grabbed Tucker around a leg. "Anything! Anything you want—Cadillac, blond, my *fortune!* Just give me this game! Please oh please . . ."

"Get this crazy dude off me!" Tucker finally shook him off his leg. "Hey, ref, who is this crazy fool?"

"Guards!" the ref bellowed. "Get this turkey outta here! Can't you control *anybody?*"

The guards pounced on Halsey and dragged him off the floor and out.

The ref raised his eyes high. "What would it actually

take to get this game going? I've never actually *prayed* before . . ."

Finally the ref handed the ball to Tucker who was to pass it in to resume play.

The Pisces on the floor were Moses, Driftwood, Jackson, Setshot, and Truth. The power was with them. They were ready to play.

Tucker fired the ball in to Nixon who dribbled to the top of the key, Truth on him like glue. Setshot double-teamed him and they stole the ball.

The Pisces worked it downcourt. Setshot took the ball and readied a shot from twenty-five feet. But he faked the shot and bounced a pass to the cutting Moses who floated in for the dunk.

"MO-SES! MO-SES!" chanted the crowd. The Pisces were coming back.

Driftwood intercepted a long pass at midcourt, found Moses cutting again for the basket, and fed him perfectly for the lay-up.

The Pisces' switching defense was suddenly impenetrable, and the Lakers couldn't get a shot off before the 24-second clock ran out.

Jackson ducked under Kareem for a score at the other end.

Tyrone was perched on the arm of Mona's chair. Her chin propped in her hand, Mona was leaning forward, calmly watching developments. "When I did my calculations earlier," she said to Tyrone, "I knew that the Pisces coudn't win tonight. Too bad they couldn't have played tomorrow. But . . ."

"But what?" Tyrone smiled at her. "Thing is, *I* know they can't win tonight, and *you* know that, but . . ." he pointed to the court, "*they* don't know that!"

Breaking into a smile, Mona gave Tyrone a hug. With mock seriousness, she said, "Tyrone, there's the hand of destiny in all this."

"Give me five!" He held out his palms, and she slapped them.

Then their eyes went to the scoreboard clock, which read 11:46. They stood up to wave their fists and cheer the team on. And the Pisces continued to play as if the presence of Mona made some mystical difference.

The Lakers did not collapse. But the Pisces kept working harder and harder, gaining with each minute.

With less than a minute to play, L.A. led, 103–97.

Moses dribbled out from the corner to hand the ball to Setshot. "Gimme a three count," he whispered, "then put her up!"

Setshot was thirty feet from the basket. Moses took off, Setshot pumped up a two-hander.

It was off to the left, but Moses was right there. He timed his leap perfectly, grabbed it and stuffed it into the rim with one smooth move.

Jackson fouled Kareem, trying to stop the sky-hook. Kareem made one of two—104–99.

Truth brought it quickly across the line and gave it off to Moses.

Moses squared off with Tucker at the top of the key, holding the ball in one hand behind his back. Suddenly he took a quick step to his left, spun back around to his right, soaring past Tucker, up even over the reach of Kareem, and slammed it in—104–101.

The crowd went wild. "MO-SES! MO-SES! . . ."

Mona opened her strongbox and scattered all her charts into the air like confetti. "Oh mighty Pisces!" she yelled ecstatically.

With twenty-seven seconds left, L.A. took the ball out. The Pisces were double-teaming and triple-teaming whoever had the ball. Over the incessant roar of the crowd, nothing could be heard on the court—not even the bouncing of the ball.

The Lakers were playing keep-away, passing the ball around to run the game clock out.

Finally, with the 24-second clock down to eight seconds, they passed in to Kareem. Kareem turned to his left to go for the hook.

But Moses cut across the key and slapped the ball away cleanly before Kareem could raise it over his head.

Moses snatched the ball up without the slightest pause and took off downcourt all the way for the stuff —104–103.

Four seconds left. The teams scrambled for position for the Lakers' crucial inbounds play. Tucker held the ball high over his head, looking for somebody to pass to. Finally he threw, intended for Kareem.

But Jackson deflected it. He and Tucker dove for it, and other players piled on top.

The ref called a jump ball.

Two seconds left.

Tucker and Jackson went up—Jackson mustering all his strength and winning the tip.

Moses grabbed it. From thirty feet, he jumped and fired. The buzzer sounded. The ball swished through. The Pisces had won, 105–104.

The rest was bedlam. The Pisces swarmed at the bench, hugging each other, hugging Mona, hugging Tyrone, slapping heads and backs. While the Lakers slunk off the floor, the crowd poured onto the court, surrounding the Pisces in the crush.

Mona climbed up on her chair to keep from being squashed, Tyrone right beside her. "Tyrone, they've beaten the charts!"

"And L.A. in the process!"

Brockington was weeping with joy.

Tilson smiled beatifically as he held out a basketball. "Anybody care to autograph this for me?"

Moses slipped out of the mob to hug Toby, who was crying with joy. Rev. Jackson stepped up to them. He clasped his hands in front of him. "Just say the magic word and I'll perform the ceremony."

Mona jumped in. "But not on the tenth or eleventh," she blustered. "Mercury's in retrograde and there's a full moon on top of it!"

"Full moons, retrogrades," Moses yelped. "We're gonna say the word anyway!"

Toby hugged him tighter. "But we haven't even got a—"

Bullet wedged in, rubbing his hands and then producing from behind Toby's ear a gold wedding band.

"Now we do!" Moses sang.

"Bullet, Bullet," Tyrone cried, slipping in under his arm, "your magic's so beautiful—if only you could talk!"

Bullet held up a hand. *"Action* speaks louder than words!"

Everybody stood stunned, then burst into laughter.

Moses raised his eyes to the clock. It read 11:59. He smiled over at Mona. Mona shrugged, smiling back devilishly. "Anybody can make a mistake."

"Ain't *nobody* made *no* mistakes," Moses said softly, holding Toby tight to him and watching the happy crowd flood the exits. "Right, Tyrone?"

"You got it, Moses!"

They slapped palms all around, and the team, along with Tyrone and Brockington and Mona and Toby and Tilson and the rest, all linked arms and headed for the tunnel.

ABOUT THE AUTHOR

RICHARD WOODLEY wrote the novel based on the screen-play for *The Bad News Bears* and its two sequels, as well as *Slapshot,* and *The Champ.* A former editor of *Life* magazine, he has had articles published in such magazines as *Esquire, Playboy, Rolling Stone,* and *Atlantic Monthly,* and has published two books of non-fiction. A resident of Manhattan, Richard Woodley is currently at work on a new novel.